Sylvan Investigations

Miles to Go
&
Promises to Keep

Sylvan Investigations

Miles to Go

&

Promises to Keep

by

Laura Anne Gilman

Plus One Press
San Francisco

Plus One Press
www.plusonepress.com

SYLVAN INVESTIGATIONS: MILES TO GO & PROMISES TO KEEP. Copyright © 2013 by Laura Anne Gilman. All rights reserved, including the right to reproduce this book or portions thereof in any form whatsoever. For information, address Plus One Press, 2885 Golden Gate Avenue, San Francisco, California, 94118.

"Miles to Go", © 2013 by Laura Anne Gilman,
 first appeared in first appeared in an eBook edition by Book View Café, October, 2013.

"Promises to Keep", © 2013 by Laura Anne Gilman,
 first appeared in first appeared in an eBook edition by Book View Café, October, 2013.

For rights information/permissions, contact rights@lauraannegilman.net

Cover designs © 2013 Tiara Lynn Agresta. For more of Tiara's work, please visit her website at tiarala.carbonmade.com

978-0-9860085-8-0
0-9860085-8-3

Library of Congress Control Number: 2013919730

First Print Edition: November, 2013

10 9 8 7 6 5 4 3 2 1

Acknowledgements

With thanks to the Early Patrons and meerkat minions

For everyone who gave me needed information about non-traditional, non-twelve step recovery and treatment programs and trends in current thinking, my heartfelt thanks.

Sylvan Investigations

Contents

Miles to Go

for Heather Fagan,
and in memory of Patricia Grogan
(1953-2007)

1

My back hurt, my horns itched, and I was pretty sure that burrito for lunch had been a mistake.

"You're bluffing," I said.

"Danny, oh Danny." The miserable fucker had the balls to smile at me. "You know I never bluff."

It was summer. Some places in the city, summer's nice. You get out by the water, maybe Orchard Beach or Coney Island, or even the Seaport if it's not too crowded, and the salt air and breeze touches your skin and you're seventeen again. And the Green, what humans called Central Park, was a blessed respite, even on the worst days.

But inside the city itself, locked within the henge of buildings that reflected heat and cast it back to the pavement which in turn shoved it up into living tissue, summer was miserable. I wanted to be somewhere with clean air, cold water, and a colder beer. Instead, I was stuck on a park bench in midtown Manhattan, watching tourists pile on and off those damn tourist buses.

The last round had been a mistake, last night. So had the first round. I'm not much for drinking—my years on the force showed me how badly that could go wrong, and my father's genetic inheritance makes me prone to…overindulgence. But an old friend was getting married next week, and the least I could do was go along with the bridal shower, make sure nobody got in trouble.

Everyone, of course, had. And now I was paying for it. At least the sweat was soaking the toxins out of my system, right?

Anderlik, next to me, smiled again. His teeth were perfectly capped, his skin naturally tanned, and his eyes flat and ugly as the pavement. His hands rested on his lap, and I noted that the creases of his pants were perfectly pressed, even in this heat. Bastard.

"So, if you're willing to negotiate, he went on, "I think we can come to an amicable position that leaves everyone satisfied."

One of the double-decker buses I'd been watching pulled up and disgorged its passengers, overwhelmed families tumbling off onto the sidewalks, fanning themselves with cheap folding fans, hats, and folded brochures, their faces red with sweat and bright with excitement. Mothers and sons, fathers and daughters, young lovers and wait for it, a pack of teenaged boys, out on a lark, not minding the heat. Sixteen, tops. They came off the bus last, already looking for their next big thrill, their body language practically screaming 'fresh meat.'

"Danny? Can we talk terms?"

I saw him then, oozing his way through the crowds like a proper snake, eyes beady and tongue practically scenting his prey in the air. Another two-three minutes, and he'd be on them, dropping lures and seeing what he could catch.

Not this time, I thought, standing up.

"Danny!"

My fist was almost an afterthought, hitting Anderlik a solid three-quarter blow on his perfect nose.

"The photos haves already gone to the PUPs," I told him. "You're going to have to negotiate with Venec. Have fun with that."

I walked off, my gaze focused on my prey, Romeo already forgotten. I moved through the crowds, aware that I was getting looks as I went. Tourists always looked; the Department of Tourism should send me a check every month. I had an actor's face, a friend once told me, and I'd be cast as Every New Yorker Ever; sardonic, weary and just a hint of amusement left in my eyes. The bastard love child of Jimmy Stewart and Woody Allen.

Slime had found his prey: he was leaning against the hip-high white barricades the DoT had put in to keep cars on the road and pedestrians on the sidewalks, his body language oozing smarter, cooler older guy. Two of the boys were buying it, the other three not so much. I'd have to wait: if they walked away, I'd have nothing, no proof. Part of me wanted them to be smart and walk away. The rest of me wanted nothing more than to get this slimy skin-seller out of business.

Something—someone—was pacing me. Tall, taller than me, dark, and female. Clearly pacing me too, with a mind to intercept, rather than just moving in the same direction I happened to be moving.

"Excuse me?"

She was talking to me, yeah. My momma raised me to be polite, most especially to women. I kept an eye on the knot of potential boy-toys ahead of me, and turned just enough to see who was trying to get my attention.

She was tall, dark, and strong-boned, with black curls pinned away from equally dark eyes and a nose like Cleopatra might've had. Not a beauty, but New York's values aren't LA's, and I've always been a sucker for an interesting face.

All right, I've always been a sucker, period.

"Danny Hendrickson, right?"

Ahead of me, Slime was leaning in, trying to close the sale. Next to me, a dark-eyed woman was calling my name.

"Honey, it's gotta wait," I said, and stepped forward. She followed.

I was a long pace away from the boys when two oversized individuals in regrettable matching outfits passed in front of me. I dodged, came around, and saw that the majority vote had won: the boys were backing away, several of them looking somewhat nervous. Good, and damn it. I stopped, and something tipped Slime off, because he looked up and saw me standing there.

He had no clue who I was, but his slimy instincts told him *what*, as much as if I'd still carried a badge. And that was enough to make him disappear like a Salamander on a frosty morning.

"Mister Hendrickson?"

I exhaled, let the irritation go, and turned to see what the hell was tapping me on the shoulder.

"Mister Hendrickson."

"Danny."

She nodded, gravely. Looking at her straight on, I could see her skin had an ashy tint to it, and she was sweating. Okay, we were all sweating, but I didn't think the heat was what had her shaking.

"My name is Ellen. Bonnie...Bonnie told me how to find you."

New York City was a big town. Bonnie knew a lot of people. But there was only one Ellen I knew about, who Bonnie Torres might have sent my way.

I'd heard about Ellen. Heard enough to be damn cautious.

She licked her lips, and raised those scared eyes to mine, and said the words that were always my damned downfall.

"I need your help."

One of these days, those words were going to get me killed. Might even be today.

We decamped to the nearest coffeehouse that wasn't Starbucks, which in this case was the venerable Café Cafee. It's been around since 1952, and looks it. Even the repeated clean-ups and gussy-ups of Times Square couldn't touch CC's.

She wrapped her hands around her coffee mug like it was the last source of warmth in a stone-cold winter. She had long fingers, broad palms, the kind of hands that looked capable, like they could saw a body apart or sew it back together, whichever she had a mind to.

She looked, in fact, like a sturdy, well-built girl, the kind who took up wall climbing or hiking, something physical, was maybe too chunky as a teenager, and has been turning it to muscle ever since.

She didn't look dangerous.

I'd heard enough to know better.

Ellen. No last name, no known background that anyone had heard of, suddenly appearing thirteen-fourteen months ago on the scene in the company of Bonnie Torres and her crew.

The so-called CSI of the magical community excelled at digging out details—and keeping those details to themselves. So I didn't ask. None of my business, no matter how curious I'd been.

And then a few weeks later, The Wren, one of the most powerful Talent currently alive on the East Coast, had taken this unknown girl to mentor. Gossip had flared immediately, of course. But when young Ellen didn't seem to be moving in her mentor's larcenous footsteps, nor in fact, doing much of note at all, the talk turned to more interesting, immediate things.

I hadn't pried, but I hadn't forgotten, either. Sudden changes and unexplained actions were relevant to my interests. Lines of mentorship were incredibly important to the Talent community, more so than blood. Why had the Wren—Genevieve Valere—

taken an unknown Talent to mentor, seemingly out of the blue? Something hadn't quite added up, knowing both Bonnie and Wren the way I did. The two of them taking an interest in this girl meant something.

What a little careful poking around turned up was that Miss Ellen No Last Name had no training, hadn't even known she as a Talent until recently, and that fact made the PUPs, Bonnie included, nervous as hell. That, to a trained investigator like, say, myself, meant that Miss Ellen also had power. Power that The Wren had been asked to shape—or control.

And now powerful Miss Ellen had come looking for me.

I suddenly wished for a shot of something stronger than caffeine to pour into my coffee.

If I was nervous, Miss Ellen was clearly terrified, but she wasn't going to let that stop her.

"Bonnie said…she said you help people."

She was too young to get the pop culture reference that went through my head, so I kept my mouth shut, nodded, and waited.

"There… someone needs your help. I just don't know *who.*"

All right: that was a different song than I usually got. I leaned back, stretched my legs out in front of me, and studied my damsel in distress. I'd gotten pretty good at judging human ages: she was twenty-three, tops. Maybe only twenty-one. Legal, by the Null world's standards. But to the Cosa Nostradamus, she was a Talent in mentorship, and that made her, in all the ways that counted, a minor.

"You know they need help, but not who it is that needs my help." Being a PI wasn't all that different from my years as a beat cop: sometimes you had to walk people through it before they'd get to the point and tell you what they wanted you to know. Small words and long silences worked better than trying to ask questions before they were ready.

"You know who I am."

It wasn't a question. She'd been in this world long enough to know that the *Cosa* gossiped like a granny on meth.

"You don't know what I am."

"Talent." A human with the ability to manipulate current, also known as magic. That was a no-brainer: human Nulls weren't part of the *Cosa Nostradamus*. Most of them didn't even know we existed.

My mother had been a sensitive Null, aware but not part of. My father... we don't talk about, much. Ever.

"I don't know anything about that. I don't know anything about any of it. Genevieve's been trying to teach me, but..." Genevieve, huh? Most days I forgot that was Wren's legal name. She swallowed, gathering courage, and I could feel something cold touch the base of my spine. Here it came, whatever it was.

"I see dead people."

Whatever I'd been expecting, it wasn't that.

"You mean like Bruce Willis?" The words just slipped out; my mouth is like that sometimes.

Ellen had a touch of steel to her little-girl-lost routine; the glare she gave me over that proud nose would have made my momma proud.

"I see people who are going to die," she clarified. "In the current. I don't ask for it, it just... comes."

"And you saw someone."

She nodded.

"Someone you know?"

She shook her head, and then hesitated, nodded.

I took a deep breath, let it out. "You saw me."

She nodded again.

"Just me?" I doubted it, and I was right

"No. There were others. But that doesn't mean... I don't know how to read what I see yet. Bonnie uses scrying crystals, but she says my visions aren't like hers. They're… more. She says I'm a–"

That sound you heard, the crystalline ping of a penny dropping? Yeah. "You're a storm seer."

She nodded, looking miserable. I didn't blame her.

No wonder they'd been keeping her quiet. The only reason I knew about storm seers was because my mother, once she figured out about my old man, got her hands on everything she could find about the *Cosa Nostradamus*, which included a lot of junk but also some of the real histories, all the way back to Founder Ben's time. Ben Franklin had codified the laws of current, helped shift it from some random hobledygook of superstition and woo-woo into a practical system that could be studied and ordered. For humans, anyway. The fatae—the non-humans—didn't use magic, they *were* magic. So it was different for them.

I was half-human, half-fatae. Didn't happen too often. Most of the time, a woman found herself with a fatae child, she drowned it, if she couldn't take care of the problem beforehand. My mother had made a different choice. I didn't think she regretted it, but I never asked, and she never told me.

If she'd asked me, I might have chosen differently, but, well.

This wasn't about me, it was about the woman sitting in front of me.

Storm seers, according to what I'd read, were a legend.

See, magic exists, but it's cranky. It doesn't like being touched, and most humans try to manipulate it, it'll fry them up like bacon. But some humans, they've got the gift. Talent. That's what they have and that's what they're called, and they're the rest of the *Cosa Nostradamus*, along with the non-humans of the world. I'd grown up with Talent, counted most of my friends among them, but they were a mystery to me, in a lot of ways.

A storm seer was that mystery wrapped around dynamite. A

storm seer, according to legends, could take wild current, the magic that hums throughout the world, emerging from the core of the earth or coming down from the sky in lightning, and see what was coming. Cassandra-style seeing, not just a touch of kenning or precog.

And apparently, what my girl saw, was death.

Specifically and relevant to my interests, *my* death.

Ellen had thought he would be...scarier. Or larger. Or not seem so...human. In her vision, her kenning, Bonnie called it, his face had been more drawn, his cheekbones more pronounced, and his chin—clean-shaven now—covered with stubble. And his horns...

You couldn't see his horns, now. His brown hair was a tousled mess, curly but not in any kind of styled way, more like he washed it and dried it and then forgot he had it, and you had to look carefully to see the tiny curved points peeking out.

About the size of her thumb, she figured. Maybe smaller: she had large hands. But very real.

Faun. Half-faun, Bonnie had said. Fatae—not human. That still blew her mind; she'd only just learned that the *things* she kept seeing out of the corner of her eyes were real, that the *things* she saw and felt and could do were real. After twenty years of being told she was imagining things, and then being told that she was crazy, reality didn't quite feel real to her.

She knew enough not to reach out and touch those half-hidden horns, though. She wanted to. Badly. Badly enough that her immediate suspicion was that it wasn't her wanting, exactly.

"Danny's a heartbreaker," Bonnie had said that morning, casually, like it wasn't anything important. "It's the whole faun thing. He can't help it."

Ellen licked her lips, and tried to focus on the vision that had sent her here. But that didn't help any, either. Her visions scared

13

the fuck out of her, more and worse than anything else. Especially now that she knew they weren't just bad dreams or hallucinations, that she wasn't crazy, and it was all real. Everyone she saw dead, died.

"Not all."

"What?" He looked at her, and she realized suddenly that she's said it out loud. She swallowed, and it felt like something sharp was stuck inside her throat.

"Not everyone I see, the ones who call to me, dies. I'm fifty-fifty, so far."

"Well. That's reassuring." He didn't sound reassured. But he also wasn't trying to pretend he was reassured, the way everyone else did. Genevieve and Sergei, even Bonnie and the others, they all tiptoed around her, careful and cautious, and she knew why. It was because she came late to this, to knowing she was a Talent, and she was supposed to have learned all that before, when she was a kid, and she didn't and that was bad.

"I saw you." She had to get it out before she was too scared to talk. "Last night. You were wet, like…like you'd gotten caught in the rain. And you looked really tired. And there were these …" she fumbled, trying to remember the details of the vision from nearly twenty four hours before. "Kids? Teenagers. Three of them. Behind you. They were all wet too, and they looked weird, but I can't tell you how. And you were all dead."

There was something in his expression when she started to describe the other people she'd seen. Like he didn't much care about himself being dead, but other people bothered him.

She understood that.

"First, relax," he said, leaning forward a little. "You're not going to be able to remember anything important if you're tensed up and stressing about remembering the important things."

He had a nice voice. Not too deep, but broad and warm, like…

14

like… she didn't know what it was like, but the voice more than the words helped her muscles loosen, her stomach unclench, and she leaned back into the booth, resting her hands on the table, even though her fingers remained clasped together maybe a little too tight.

"Tell me about where you were, before."

"Before?"

"Before you saw me. Where were you?"

She had been in Wren's living room. They were supposed to be having a class—she thought it was a class, anyway. Mostly, it was Wren telling stories, stuff that happened to her, or to her mentor. Sometimes older stories, about things that happened hundreds of years ago. The sky had been clear that morning, a sharp blue, with only a hint of clouds when she walked from her little studio apartment uptown to where her mentor lived. The air had felt…strange, sort of tingly, but there was so much that was new to her, she hadn't thought anything of it.

"Wren was telling me about how she learned about being a Retriever. About how her no-see-me was part of her, and since she couldn't turn it off, she had to learn to use it."

That story, at least, had been obvious. She might be new to this, and kind of clueless about magic, but she wasn't dumb. Being a storm-seer was part of who she was, and she couldn't shut it off, either. So she had to live with it, or…

"And then… I felt weird. Like I had too much to drink, or like the building was moving under me, moving and spinning. And thunder cracked, right overhead, even though it hadn't been raining, and I heard Wren swear, and then everything went black, like it does when a movie's about to start, and I saw…" she remembered what Bonnie had told her that first time, about stepping back from what she saw. "I saw a figure, a man, stepping forward. Ordinary clothes, jeans and a T-shirt, a red T-shirt. And soaking wet. The way you get when you're caught in a storm, and your umbrella gets trashed by the wind. Tired. He looked tired, and worried, and there was a streak of something on his face, something... blood."

She hadn't remembered that before, but now it was clear as that first vision, a streak of muddy brown from ear to chin. Not a scratch, more like he'd tried to wipe his face and smeared it off his hands.

"And horns. I remember the horns. Your hair was matted, and they showed through, and I said something to you about it and you were annoyed and then the others appeared."

She hadn't remembered that at first, either. Had it happened in her original vision, that sense of being there, of knowing him, or speaking to him? Or was it coming up now because she knew him, had spoken to him? She didn't know.

Too much she didn't know, and only one thing she did for sure.

"Three teenagers. Two girls and a boy. All wet, and tired, and.... I don't know. I can't see them as clearly, they're already fading. There's something about them, something strange. It's like something's taking bites out of them? Something hungry, nibbling." Her voice faded for a moment, then came back, stronger. "Mouths of steel biting at them, a bite at a time. But that might be a metaphor. I still don't know how this works, exactly. At all. But they're angry, not scared. Really angry."

"Who are they angry at?"

Ellen shivered. "I don't know."

She tried to hold onto the vision, try to wring something more out of it, prove she could be good at this, but it was fading, the split-second of clarity gone.

"That's all. I had the vision, and then the rain came down like crazy, and it was gone."

Lightning triggered it. Not lightning itself, but the energy within

16

the lightning, the current—magic—that ran through every bit of electricity in the world, her brain reacting to it somehow. That was what they told her. That's why they called her a storm-seer.

"I didn't sense the storm coming," she said to herself. "I wasn't ready. I need to learn how to be ready."

She felt her hands covered by something warmer, and opened her eyes to see his hands on hers, the skin several shades lighter, but the flesh so much warmer. She was cold all over, all the way down to her bones.

"It takes time," he said. "You did great. Thank you."

Then, as though he'd just realized he was touching her, his hands were gone, his arms crossed over his chest, and he was looking away, calling the waitress over for more coffee that she didn't want, but took anyway, because that made the mug warm enough to hold, warm enough to rewarm her.

"I don't know where, or when, though," she said. "Or who. Last time…"

Last time, she had seen her mentor, whom she knew now, but not then. And the man who had died, Bonnie's boss, whom she had never met, but they had known, the minute she described him. She'd told them he was going to die, and then he did.

"You've known about what you are for, what, a year? Less? And this is your second storm vision?" He sounded like he was making notes, even though he didn't write anything down.

"My third." The second one had been induced, her mentor calling down lightning—the most terrifying experience she'd ever had, including visions, had been standing on the rooftop watching that happen—and she'd seen half a dozen people, but none of them had called out to her. None of them had forced her to find someone, and tell what she had seen.

Genevieve had said that maybe those were natural deaths, or older deaths that had already happened, or a dozen things that

17

were supposed to make her feel better, that maybe not every vision she'd have would involve terrible things.

But those people were still dead, or going to die. And she couldn't do anything about it.

"Third. And you're handling them—upright, sane, and still verbal. I'd say you've got nothing to be ashamed of."

When Sergei, Genevieve's partner, said things like that, she knew he was trying to make her feel better. When her mentor said it, she was trying to build up her confidence, make her willing to try another test, learn another thing, listen to another story. And both those things were...nice. No, more than nice. After a lifetime of people -her own family- thinking she was lying, or crazy, the reassurances were a lifeline, and Ellen was smart enough to grab on with both hands.

But this man... he said it casually, almost off-handedly. Like of *course* she was managing it. Ellen wasn't sure how to deal with that.

"They're still dead," she said. "I was only able to save one of them."

That got his attention. He looked at her—straight at her, those hazel eyes looking more green than brown, and sharp as flint—and smiled. It wasn't a particularly happy smile, though.

"That's why you came to me."

2

I'd given her my best shot, reassured her of my competence, and not quoted her a fee—this one was going to be on the house, and Bonnie had known that when she sent Valere's pet Seer to me. I'd expected the girl to gasp out some thanks, grab her bag, and flee.

Instead, she sat there, staring at me like she expected me to get up and dance, or turn into a goat, or something.

I resisted the urge to check my hair, to make sure my horns weren't showing, and waited.

"I need to see this through," she said, her voice small and uncertain. Then her jaw moved again, like she was chewing something over, and she said it again, this time stronger. "I need to see this through."

Oh. Ah, hell. I worked alone. All right, sometimes I worked with the PUPs, when they called me, or if our cases collided, the way they'd done once or twice, but on my own, my own time, I wasn't a team player. My duty sergeant had made that point clear, several times during my tenure with the NYPD. My partner had been a patient man, but when he retired… yeah. Not a team player.

19

It wasn't just about having to hide what I was, either. Since leaving the force I'd been more or less out—not that I'd been all that "in" back then, either. I liked my space, mental and physical.

I could probably say Boo! and she'd run. She had that edge-of-skin look to her, like she was terrified but holding on through sheer grit.

Damn it. I respected grit. I thought it was dumber'n hell, but I respected it.

And if she was seeing that scene play out behind her eyes...

I knew something about that, too.

"You need me," she said, her voice desperate and a little too fast. "I know what they look like. I know..."

"It's all right, girl," I said, not even pretending to be happy about it. "You don't have to convince me. If I say no you're just going to get into mischief on your own, probably, and then I'm going to have The Wren breathing down my neck, and no thank you."

Bonnie I could sweet talk and explain. Wren Valere...

Valere scared me, just a little. I had no shame in admitting that. Valere was a little crazy herself, where it mattered.

"I won't be any trouble," she promised. I gave that the once-over it deserved, and she blushed, her cheeks darkening like she knew it was a promise she was bound to break.

"I need you to agree to three things, though." I pulled my cop voice out from the box I'd shoved it in, fixing her with the "don't make me tell your parents" look that my old partner had perfected after two decades on the street. "One, that no matter what I say, no matter how it sounds, if I tell you to do something, you do it."

A single wisecrack or hesitation, and I'd hog tie her and deliver her to Wren's front door, if I had to.

She nodded.

"Two, if I decide, for any reason, that I'm doing something alone, you accept that, without back talk."

She nodded again, although with a faint hesitation. I wasn't sure I'd have believed her, if she'd agreed without hesitation. I love women, individually and as a gender, but there wasn't a one of them that accepted anything without argument. Most days, I counted that a plus, but not on the job.

"Three. You don't use current unless you clear it with me. I know you Talent, you do it like breathing, but the people we're talking to, they're not always comfortable with it, and I can't have you spooking them, or pissing them off."

I didn't expect her laugh, and didn't expect it to sound so...sweet.

"That, I can promise," she said.

Right. She was new to all this. Current probably still freaked her out worse than it did a half-headblind Null.

"Good," I said, dropping the bad cop routine. "Let's go."

I threw enough cash on the table to cover the coffee, and stood up. She took longer to unfold herself—she was taller than me, if only by an inch or so, but it was mostly leg, like watching a giraffe find its balance, except that made her sound ungainly and she wasn't. Just... unsure.

Useless in a fight, I decided. Hopefully, it wasn't going to come to that. She'd seen me dead, not herself.

Me, and three teenagers.

If Bonnie were here, she'd point out, logically, that I might not be in danger at all if I walked away. Yeah. It wasn't a choice: I'd do whatever it took to find out who those kids were, where they were, and how to get them out of whatever danger they were in.

Bonnie knew that. Anyone who knew me, knew that.

Outside the coffee shop, I held up a hand, and then pointed with two fingers. "Go stand over there."

She looked puzzled, but did as I said, just like she'd promised. Once she was a safe distance away, I pulled out my cell phone, and turned it on. Hanging around Talent as often as I did, you learned to power down your electronics when you weren't using them, just in case. Current might run with electricity, but they didn't like sharing the same track, and current usually won

I hit number three on my contact list, and waited until the other man picked up.

"Didier. It's Hendrickson." Not that Sergei Didier answered his phone without knowing full well who was on the other side, but my momma had drilled manners into me. "Just wanted to let you and your bird know that I've got possession of your fledgling."

"Good." Didier was his usual urbane self, but I'd known the human long enough to be able to detect relief in that smooth voice. "I assume she has told you what is bothering her?"

"Oh yes. I've decided to take the case."

"I thought that you might." There was a pause, almost imperceptible. "And I should tell Genevieve that her student will be available for lessons, or is she otherwise engaged?"

That got a laugh out of me. "She's determined to play hooky." I slid a glance at her. She was still waiting, patient the way people who've spent a lot of their life waiting get. Her hands were at her sides, not fiddling with anything, her eyes were soft and her face almost relaxed. She looked almost passive, but I could feel the tension in her body. It was just coiled down deep, and under an almost scary level of control. Whatever I might have to worry about her current, leak wasn't going to be part of it.

"Danny." And there was Wren on the other end of the line: even if I hadn't known, the static filling the spaces between words a dead giveaway. A Talent, agitated, near electronics. I hoped Didier had a spare phone handy.

"Valere."

"She shouldn't be out and about."

22

If half of what I'd heard and suspected was true, Valere was right about that. "She's invested in this. I send her back with a pat on her head, tell her not to worry about it…. How well would you have taken to that?"

There was a long, dire silence; even the static went dead. Then: "You take care of her, Danny. Keep her safe."

I closed my eyes, feeling an impossible weariness wrap itself around me, all the way down to my bones. It was a too-familiar feeling, these days. I didn't need a shrink to tell me I was on the edge of burnout. For every kid I found and brought home, five more went missing. I was starting to wonder if any one person could really make a difference. But making a difference was the only sanity I had.

"Understood, Valere."

I ended the call, turned off the phone, and put it back in my pocket. I turned and studied my new temporary companion. She looked back at me, still waiting. Tall, yeah, and not lean, and not graceful exactly, but there was power coiled under there, like the lacrosse players I'd see out in the Green, sometimes, or the field hockey girls. Potential, that was the word I'd been looking for.

"What do you see?" she asked, finally. Her voice carried without stress across the sidewalk, despite the usual ceaseless noise of traffic and sirens and the construction they were still doing up on 53rd.

"Trouble," I said honestly.

For some reason, that seemed to please her.

Ellen knew it was rude to stare—and in this world she'd fallen into probably dangerous—but she couldn't stop herself from looking at him, even if she had to turn away every time he looked back, like some dumb, giggling teenager. His words—she shouldn't feel flattered by them. She'd worked so hard, all her life, not to be trouble, to stay out of trouble, not give anyone—her parents, her teachers, the few friends she could keep—cause to turn away, that his words should have hurt.

But he wasn't like her parents, or her teachers. He wasn't even like the other Talent, not the woman who had lured her away with promises of being "special" and then abandoned her, not even like Bonnie and Genevieve and the others, the ones who were showing her how to use current, teaching her how to control it. And he wasn't *normal*, wasn't…what did Genevieve call them? Wasn't a Null, thinking that she was crazy because she saw things, felt things, they didn't.

He wasn't human. Like the…the other things, the things she saw out of the corner of her eye, the ones Wren said were called fatae. They were real, she wasn't crazy. But most of them were…. Too weird. He looked human, if you didn't see the horns, or look too closely at his face, the way his ears weren't quite rounded, and his cheekbones were too high.

But his eyes were kind, and his voice was soft, even when he was obviously annoyed, and there was something about him that made her feel like for once, she didn't have to be careful, that she wasn't going to break something, ruin everything.

That he wouldn't turn away, no matter how badly she fucked up.

Ellen didn't trust that feeling. But when he called her trouble, it felt like…like something that didn't hurt.

And maybe, she didn't quite dare to think, if she could help him, if her vision saved those lives, saved *his* life….

She couldn't think that far, what that might mean

The home base of Sylvan Investigations wasn't all that, but it was in a good enough part of Manhattan to reassure clients, and a boring enough part of town that I could afford the rent without dipping into my pitiful excuse for a pension. Mostly.

24

My shadow looked around the front room without a comment. I tried to see it through her eyes: windowless, painted an allegedly-soothing shade of cream that wasn't aging well, two broad-leafed plants in the corner that needed repotting already. There was a wooden secretary's desk dead center, three-quarters of the way back, with a scattering of papers and a hand-sized intercom system set-up, even though I'd never hired a secretary in my entire career. The look, overall, was bare bones, but that was okay: the people who hired me weren't looking for pretty. They wanted competence.

Shadow finished sizing the place up, and if she had an opinion, she didn't show it. "What now?" she asked.

"Now, we go to work. Or rather, I do. You're going to be useless right now." I meant it jokingly, but the expression on her face reminded me that this wasn't Bonnie I was talking to—I had to watch myself, watch my words.

"You know about current, and electricity?"

She bit her lip, and was obviously thinking carefully about what to say. Good. Caution wasn't a bad trick. "Current and electricity run together, come from the same sources, have a lot of the same properties. We—Talent—can channel both of them, they won't harm us, but current's the one we can shape and use. It's the stuff they used to call magic in the old days."

"Yeah. Which means that you people are pretty much shit out of luck when it comes to things like computers, because that ability to channel also means you're walking talking lightning rods. But I find them, computers, damned useful in my job."

"So what do I do?"

I nodded at the secretary's desk. "There's a pad of paper, and pencils, maybe even a pen with ink. Sit down and write out everything, and I mean *everything* you can remember from your visions. Visuals, feelings, hell, even what you were tasting in your mouth at the time."

25

"You think that's important?"

"I don't know that it's not."

She considered that, letting it settle in her brain before nodding. I was starting to like the girl, she had a solid brain between her ears. With Valere's mentoring and Bonnie's guidance, she just might make it.

"You want coffee?" I asked. "The machine's old, but it does decent enough work."

"I don't drink coffee," she said, and my opinion dropped a little. I also wondered how the hell she was surviving, living with Valere. Maybe she teamed up with Didier and drank tea?

"I like my caffeine carbonated," she said, almost apologetically.

"Oh, right. There's some soda in the fridge but I don't know how old it is. Does that stuff go bad?"

"Not that my taste buds ever noticed." She went to the little fridge tucked under the far counter, and pulled out a can, frowning at it. "Yeah, that'll do."

My obligations dealt with, I opened the door to the back office, and went in. I left the door open, just in case.

I'd upgraded to a sweet little laptop a few months ago, which was one of the reasons I was leery of letting a Talent—especially an untrained one—anywhere near it. The older desktops were easier to ground. Nick, one of Bonnie's teammates, said that netbooks were actually safer around Talent—he used one, when he did his Talent-hacking thing—but my hands never fit on the keyboards.

"All right, Chinjy, give me what you've got."

The Child in Jeopardy site was a relatively recent thing, compiling every Amber alert, every state's child welfare filing, every missing person's report filed on a minor, swept and sorted into a database that could be broken down by gender, location, description, and type of abduction, and multiples of same. You had to be licensed and accredited to get access, hoops upon hoops set in place to prevent abuse and satisfy the privacy rights advocates. But the retrieval rate for missing minors had gone up seven percent since we—private investigators and other non-government interests—were able to use it, and that made all the hoops, and the yearly fee, worth it to me.

The sheer number of names in the database always made me want to drink. I'd learned to do a tunnel vision sort of thing, only look at the ones who fell within the parameters of my case, and never, ever for fucking ever look when I wasn't on a case. I focused on the girls, narrowed down the parameters, and still got over thirty kickbacks just in the past six months. I needed more.

"Hey–" and for a second I couldn't remember her name, only "Shadow" and I didn't think that would go over well. But before I could remember, she was in the doorway, hesitant, like she wasn't sure she was allowed in.

Computer. Right. I'd warned her off.

"How you coming with those notes?" I asked.

She held up the pad, and I could see that it had been filled with writing and a not-bad pencil sketch of three faces. "The moment I started, it all kind of fell out."

"Talk to me. What's most significant, most memorable about them?"

She hesitated, and I realized that her body language wasn't just about proximity to the computer, or me. Something else was going on. Then something clicked for her, you could see it in her face. "What?"

It took a second for her to put the thought into words. "The kids. The ones I saw. They... their skin color was off, and it threw me. I'd thought there was a scrim between us, or they were blue from the cold, but the more I tried to remember, the more I... their skin was weird. And they had gills. On their necks." She raised her hand and placed it on the side of her own neck, like you would if something bit you.

Well, hell. I closed the laptop and stood up, palming the taser stashed in the desk drawer. "Right. Time to do a different kind of research."

3

I felt bad, dragging Shadow everywhere, but I didn't even suggest her staying back in the office. First, I was under orders to keep her safe, and while I didn't think anything was going to go down in my office—I'd been working there for six years now and the most excitement we'd ever had was when a rabid squirrel decided to take up residence in the bathroom down the hall—I couldn't say for sure trouble *wasn't* going to suddenly show up.

And anyway, she wasn't going to stay put, not when we might have a lead on the missing kids. I knew that already. She might be a mouse, but if you poked her, she roared.

We took the 5 line downtown. It was the start of rush hour, so we didn't catch seats, but there was room to railhang without getting squashed up against other people. I'm a New Yorker through and through but I hate the subway, especially when it's crowded. People tend to cluster toward me, not even realizing it, and I've got a touch of clausto to begin with. My mom might've spent most of her career before me on a ship, but my fatae genetics were geared more to open hillsides and relative solitude. I never did understand why I stayed in New York, except I couldn't quite wrap my horns around leaving.

Shadow swayed a bit, swinging toward me, then catching herself. She had that slightly dreamy look on her face, one I recognized from long exposure: she was jamming with the current that ran through the underground tracks, looping around the electricity that powered the trains, the lights, streaming through stone-carved tunnels, winding in around itself and just waiting for a Talent to come siphon it off, just a little bit, a hit to sooth the stress of a long day.

Or so I'd been told. All I could feel was the rackety-clack of the rail under us, the occasional hitching scream of the brakes, and random cold bursts of the train's straining air conditioning. But it was nice to watch her face, see the tiny stress lines around her mouth ease. She had a nice mouth, wide, and full, but not pouty or posed. You could describe it in crude terms, yeah, but my mother did her best to raise me to not be a dick. Anyway, all I could think was that she probably had an awesome smile. If she ever smiled.

"What are we—where are we going?" she asked, not opening her eyes.

"What, you're not going to just trail after me like a good shadow, trusting my decision-making?" The moment the words fell out of my mouth I wished I could recall them, remembering how badly she'd reacted before. Her eyes opened then, and she stared at me, judging something.

I guess I passed, because she shook her head, and closed her eyes again, letting her body sway as we slid around a curve in the tunnel. "I don't trust anybody anymore," she said. "But I'm good at following."

There was something in that, some depth in her words that lost me. I'm usually pretty good at sounding the depths, too. I decided to focus on the hunt, and worry about my shadow later.

30

"Yeah, you proved that earlier," I admitted. "We're going to talk to some people, best you stay quiet and just pay attention. If you see anything, or you remember anything, tuck it into your brain and tell me when we're alone."

She clearly remembered her earlier promise, because she just nodded once, and followed me up out of the station at our stop, down John Street and into the chaos of the South Street Seaport. Home to some of the most comprehensive kitsch in all Manhattan, outdoing even Times Square on summer afternoons when half the world and three-quarters of Wall Street were there for the view, the booze, and the mingling. I'd spent more than a few hours here himself, killing time and a few beers, watching the tall ships and the tourist boats.

This time, I bypassed the flurry of the Seaport itself, dodging buskers, tour-hawkers, and tourists, Ellen at my heel. Under the overhang, and down past the old fish market, where the East River greenway began.

This had been easier when it was still run down and dingy; nobody questioned a guy sitting on the bench, talking to himself. But then, I wasn't by myself, now.

That would make it easier, and possibly harder.

"Sit."

She sat, legs stretched out in front of her, and damn the girl had some legs. She leaned back against the bench, her elbows braced, and lifted her face to the sun, then looked at me when I sat next to her.

"Whatever happens, just pretend I'm talking to you."

"Whatever," and she lazily waved a hand. It wasn't a perfect act, but it was pretty good. I turned so that it seemed as though I was facing her, and watched the walkway over her shoulder.

"I'm here looking for information. You know that I pay fair for whatever I get."

31

She shook her head, and smiled. Two men came along the path, talking to each other; one of them noticed her legs, the other kept yakking, and then they were gone. To my right, something in the sparse shrubbery between the walkway and the street made a rustling noise. It could have been the wind, or a squirrel, or a rat.

"Come on, don't waste my time." I played irritated, annoyed, no time to waste. Truth was, I'd be willing to sit here all night if that's what it took. I'd done it before.

"More children gone walkabye?"

My shadow jumped a little; the voice was right by her elbow, way too close, and way too loud for a whisper. I might have jumped too, if I hadn't been expecting it.

If someone weren't paying attention, they'd think that a bush had overgrown the verge, greenstick branches reaching over the bench, buds of leaves too small for full-summer and the faintest hint of fading yellow flowers. Then they'd realize that the branches were too thick, the leaves and flowers moving with a slow, steady pulse, and then, if they were paying attention, they'd see the eyes, heavy black orbs, and the small, sucker-shaped mouth.

"You know me," I said, keeping it casual. The trick to dealing with fatae was to never let them think that you needed them. Humans liked to be needed, got off on it, could be flattered into giving it away. Fatae saw it as a chance to build obligation, accumulate debt they could turn around and use for themselves.

Of course, they want to be needed, too. The desire to show off how much smarter you were is universal to every species that could communicate.

"We know you," it agreed. "Animal, vegetable, or mineral?"

"Fish," I said.

"Ah."

One branchlet touched Ellen's shoulder, and she managed not to jump or shudder. Her expression wasn't too happy, though.

32

"Talent," it said. "Shiny-sharp."

"Valere's," I said, and the branchlet paused, squeezed once, and fell away. Her eyes were wide, but she didn't react. Someday—soon, I was betting—she'd be able to singe grabby hands on her own. But for now, a mentor's protection was...well, part of why Talent had mentors.

"You have anything?" I didn't want to waste time.

"Wrong time, right place. Fish go missing, weeks ago. Think first it was prank or school-joke, but they not come back. School scared, swim back north. Think shark got 'em."

Close enough, if not the kind of sharks the school had been thinking.

"You're a pal," I said, and passed something flat-palmed over Ellen's shoulder, where it disappeared into the leaflets.

Ellen focused on breathing. If she kept breathing, she'd be all right, even when that...thing touched her, sticky-sharp pressure on her shoulder, on her neck, and she wouldn't turn around to look, didn't want to see anything more than what she'd already glimpsed out of the side of her eyes. She focused instead on Danny, on his face, his hands moving as he talked. He had nice hands, strong ones. They looked like they'd be capable of doing a lot more than hailing a cab or typing. She moved her gaze up to his face, the rough lines of his jaw, the curls plastered now in the summer heat against his forehead. He had cute ears. She noticed that in passing, not letting herself smile at the thought. His attention was on whatever was touching her, talking to it, listening to the hot whisper that she didn't dare listen to, or she would turn to look at it, and she knew if she did it would be over, she would freak, she would break her promise to Danny, and right now that promise—that she would follow, and she would tell him everything, and he'd find a way out of the nightmare of her vision, was all that was keeping her intact.

"Feel your core," Genevieve had told her. *"Reach in, down into where you feel the most centered, the most real and shove your hands into that, feel what's there."*

Ellen'd spent so many years being told she was crazy, just looking for attention, imagining things.... When the Central Park cult leader had told her she was special, that she had something, and then cast her out, Ellen had decided that they were all right, that everything she felt, everything she saw, thought she'd seen, just meant she was crazy, broken.

She still wasn't sure she wasn't. But when she breathed deep and reached, the way Genevieve had taught her, the static prickle of warmth and comfort that greeted her, stinging up her arms and spine, down her legs, connecting her to every inch of her body and the static waiting beyond....

It made her feel like broken was another word for amazing.

And then the *thing* touched her again, and her eyes went wide, instinctively falling into her core the rest of the world fading to a blur of grey sounds, wrapping herself in the static, the *current* that rested inside her, and suddenly she could see the three teens again, the blue tinge of their skin, the dampness of their clothing, the faded, haunted expression in their eyes, not hurt or angry but lost, so lost, and she needed to find them, she needed to wipe that look away and if she just reached, she knew that she could find them, could-

"Ellen."

She opened her eyes, not remembering having closed them, and Danny's hands were on hers, his face inches away, his eyes intent enough on her to be scary. The thing behind her was gone, she knew that without looking.

"It wasn't going to hurt you. It was just curious. You're strong, we can all feel that. Some of them get a little grabby, but… "

She almost couldn't remember what he was talking about. "I saw them again."

34

He pulled back, his expression changing from concern to something sharper, more hungry. "Another vision?"

"Not a new vision, it was… I saw it again, only closer, clearer. More details, things I missed last time."

"Is that normal?"

She almost cried at the absurdity of the question, and his face changed again as though realizing that yeah, she had no idea. It was subtle, something around his eyes and mouth, the way they tensed and relaxed, but she could read them like signposts, and somehow that let her breathe more easily.

"You'll remember it now, though?" he asked.

"I…yes." Before, the visions had been like nightmares, fading wisps that couldn't be clutched at, disappearing almost the moment she became aware of them. This time it was different.

Different worried her, but she thought maybe it was the way Genevieve had said, that the more control she got, the better she'd be at this, more able to control it. Control was the name of the game.

Danny stood up, slipping sunglasses back on, pushing them up the bridge of his nose and looking away, over across the water. "My snitch confirmed that several merfolk disappeared from here, so we're on the right track."

"Mer…mermaids?"

"Don't ever call 'em that if you want to step into the ocean without fear, ever again. Merfolk, or mers."

She nodded, storing that information away with everything else she'd been learning. "They disappeared from here?"

"Under this very dock, it says."

It being the ..thing that had been behind her, that had touched her. She resisted another shudder, and instead got up off the bench—noting as she did so that what she'd thought was a bush was now gone, as though it had gotten up on its roots and tip-toed

35

away—and walked across to the railing overlooking the water. Not really the ocean, here, if she remembered the maps right. The end of the East River and the start of the bay, waters mixing and mingling with the tides. She tried to imagine beings swimming underneath, living in those waters, and was surprised to find that it was easy enough. She'd already been introduced to a woman who lived in, no, *belonged to* a tree, after all. Why not mers?

"Danny?"

It was the first time she'd used my name. That was my first thought, even as I got up to join her where she stood along the railing. The slightly briny air made me even more aware of the sweat on my scalp and back, while her skin practically shimmered in the sunlight, bringing out dark copper highlights along her cheekbone. Amerindian blood in there, maybe. Or just that I don't know enough about human races to catch the clues; they were all so much alike, compared to the fatae, I found it difficult to take the divisions seriously.

"Did you remember something else?" I asked, resting my hands on the wooden railing, and looking not at her, but the ocean spread out in front of us. If I narrowed my gaze enough, I could block out the boats and the buildings, and almost imagine the city didn't exist around us, just for an instant.

"No. I...." She kept looking out across the water too, her head turning slightly, scanning from left to right, with the longest hesitation toward the right. "I can feel them."

"What?" Okay, that wasn't what I'd been expecting. I didn't know seers could do that. "When you say feel, you mean...?"

"I don't know. You, ah, you feel different. You, the...the thing that touched me, PB—all the fatae I've met so far, you all feel different, but when you're near me I can feel you, recognize you. I can feel them here, too. Or, something, anyway. Something that feels like what I saw in the vision." Her forehead crinkled again, trying to get the right words. "Mers, I guess, but specific. Familiar feels."

Talent, I'd been told, could pick up signatures, the feeling current got after it's been wrapped around another Talent, or something. But it took training, and a level of skill there was no way Shadow had, not yet. Still, she'd already had them in her head, their current, and their fate, zapped into her brain. That could be enough of a connection. Maybe.

Magic. I might be part of it, but that didn't mean I understood it. Not really. I didn't let that stop me, though.

"Can you follow it? The feeling?"

"I... yes. Maybe. Yes." Her breath hitched, and she nodded. Yeah, she could do that.

From what I'd already figured about Shadow, she didn't have a hell of a lot of self-confidence, and doubly so when it came to what she could do, what she *was*. So 'maybe-yes' was enough for me. "But we need to get out on the water. I can't follow it from here."

Oh, I so really hadn't wanted to hear that.

4

Once I'd accepted the fact that we were going to have to get our toes wet, metaphorically if hopefully not literally, we had to find a way to get out there. I considered and then discarded the idea of renting one of the two-person kayaks that people took out on the Hudson—with my luck we'd capsize and drown, and no thanks. There were half a dozen charters and ferries that worked the rivers, but they all kept to a regular route, and I wasn't going to rely on Shadow's scent trail, such as it was, sticking to regular routes. If our missing kids had been taken, odds were low it had been on a registered passenger ferry. So I went an alternative route. Or tried to, anyway.

"So, you want to hire me, but you don't know for how long, or where you want to go?" The guy leaned against the wooden sign advertising his fishing boat, and shook his head. "Sorry, no."

"It's nothing illegal. Or even immoral." I'd already showed him my PI license, but that hadn't impressed him much. To be fair, it didn't impress many people. I might look like the quintessential ideal of a New Yorker, as filtered through Hollywood, but I didn't look much like a hard-bitten PI, I guess. Maybe I should switch out the baseball cap for a fedora, or something.

"Ffffft." The captain made his opinion of illegality or immorality clear. "S'not the laws it's the cost. Fuel's too expensive to be doing that. You want to wander, you want a smaller boat. Or a sailboat."

Those were actually two things I really didn't want. But he had a point.

"Got someone in mind?" I asked. Recommendations were always useful, even if I didn't take them.

"Talk to Tal Berthiaume, captain a' the *Mercy Me*. They've got a slip up at the Basin. *Mercy Me* doesn't do charters, but you're interesting enough a request, Tal might bite."

I'd never actually been to the Boat Basin—it was out of my usual range, as far on the Upper West Side as you could get without actually hitting New Jersey. It had the usual blend of rundown and very expensive that you get at working marinas, but the view up and down the Hudson was definitely millionaire's row. I could see why people lived here, year round.

Shadow, and I needed to stop thinking of her as that before it stuck, was, well, shadowing my heels without a word, but her gaze was taking everything in. Clearly, she'd never been here before, either. "Can you imagine living on a boat?" she asked, her voice sounding younger and more gleefully innocent than it had been before.

"No." I could, actually, but it wasn't a pleasant thought. Give me a nice apartment in a nice building, where the bathroom has room to turn around, and you don't get seagulls crapping in your morning coffee.

"That's the *Mercy Me*," she said, pointing down one of the wooden extensions, clearly a lower-rent section of the Basin.

She was a sailboat. Maybe there was a technical term for the size or how many sails or whatever, but "sailboat" summed it up for me: sails the color of, well, canvas run up on masts, the ship itself trimly built, painted a dark blue, with pale yellow trim. The railings were varnished wood, and you could see the care that maintained them, even from here.

"Anyone home?" I called, as we reached its berth.

"Hang on," a voice called, and then someone appeared from below the floor—the deck.

Legs. Long legs, but not skinny, curving under shorts that came a respectable way down the thigh, connected to a torso clad in a white T-shirt, arms just as long and curved, and my gaze connected with the face that went with that body, and it was looking at me with bemused patience.

Next to me, Shadow let out an unkind snicker.

"I was told you might be agreeable to a day-hire," I said. If they thought getting caught staring was going to discomfit me, they were in for a surprise. I might not give in to the more basic urges of my faun genetics, but lack of shame was one of the things I'd found useful.

"Today? Local charter, out and back again by sunset?" When I nodded, the ship's master went on, "Cash, in advance. Five hundred. There's an ATM at the dock, if you need it."

"You don't want to know–"

"Nope. You're hiring me to take your lady on a romantic cruise around the island, that's your business. I got rent to make. The money gets you on-board, soda and water included, but if you want food you gotta bring your own. No glass, no drugs, no booze. If the cops board us and you're not clean, I'll hand you over to them without a second thought."

"Got it." I turned to Ellen, meaning to give her my ATM card and send her to get the cash out while I discussed any further terms with our captain, then realized that handing my ATM card to a Talent—a powerful and mostly untrained Talent—was one of my less thought-out ideas, unless I wanted to have to stop by the bank and get a new card after her current had demagnetized the damn thing.

"I'll be right back."

By the time I got back—after having a slight panic about leaving enough money in my account to cover the bills that would be paid in the next day or so—Ellen and our Captain had settled in, Shadow curled up on a wooden locker that was doubling as a bench, and the Captain doing competent-looking things with ropes.

I hesitated, then gave myself a hard shove, and climbed, rather inelegantly, onto the ship itself. The moment my feet hit the deck, my entire body swayed once, a slow rolling movement I felt from the soles of my feet all the way up my spine and into the back of my head, and it took every bit of stubborn I had not to turn around and get the hell *off* that boat.

My mother might have been a sailor, but water and I did not get along.

"Captain Tal says all I have to do is stand in the front of the ship and point, and she can get us there," Ellen said.

Tal—I was guessing it was short for Talia, or something—shrugged. "You're paying, you get to choose. If we start to get somewhere we shouldn't be, I'll tell you."

"I could always use some help with that," I said, not even meaning to turn on the charm, but Tal's face melted a little, the way people always did.

If I'd been full-blood, she might have offered me more than a smile. If I'd been full-blood, I wouldn't be here in the first place.

Tal Berthiaume—Tal was short for Thea Anna-Louise, Ellen

had learned while I was gone and no, the good captain apparently hadn't forgiven her parents yet—was a good sailor, and the *Mercy Me* seemed to be a good ship. I spent the first hour trying not to throw up, and the second hour wondering why I hadn't let myself throw up more often.

"You're really crap on boats, aren't you?" Ellen seemed surprised, and not inclined to tease, although I suspected it was less having to do with kindness and more not being sure how I'd react. Someone had told her to sit down and shut up a load too often, but I didn't have the energy to do any reassuring just then.

"Yeah well, I'm built for ground." I took a sip of the ginger ale Tal had provided, trying to ignore the rise and dip of the boat as we cut through the water. We couldn't go exactly the direction Ellen pointed at, but the winds seemed to be behaving, far as I could tell, taking us sideways in the direction we wanted.

If all else failed, we'd been told, there was an engine that would get us there.

"Landlubber?" Tal had used that phrase first, less kindly than Ellen did.

"I'm half-faun." She knew I wasn't human, but she was still learning the *Cosa Nostradamus*, and even Talent had trouble with all the various breeds. Hell, I wasn't sure I could name them all, and it was my *job* to know 'em. "Named for the god Faunus, although we could just as easily have taken Pan's name. Woodland revels are more our thing, not seaborne hijinks."

Woodland revels, meaning indulgences of all sorts, especially sex. The few cousins I'd met over the years took the "life is a party" philosophy to heart and groin, and they were charming enough to make humans—and a lot of other fatae—go along with them. Unfortunately, they matched charm with an utter and absolute inability to think about consequences, long or short term.

I didn't spend a lot of time with my cousins.

42

The *Mercy Me* hit another swell, and I had to interrupt my explanation with another bolt for the bucket.

"Nice impression you're getting of me," I said wearily. I'd done worse, in front of more people—the first dead body we found on my first month on the job, in mid-summer, was high up there—but this wasn't so good for my ego, either.

"Actually, it is kind of nice," Ellen said. "Everyone I've met in the city so far is so… competent. It's unnerving." She swallowed, her throat working visibly, and looked away, like she thought she'd said too much and didn't know how to take it back.

I just laughed. "Yeah. Seeing as who you've been hanging with, I can imagine the competence level has been nauseatingly high." Maybe I should have used another word… but no, my stomach stayed quiet for the moment. "If it helps any, Valere unnerves *everyone.*"

"She didn't want to take me. I know that. I don't know why–" She broke off what she was saying, coming to point like a rescue dog catching scent of a live one.

"There."

I followed where she was looking, and sighed. "South Jersey. Well, could have been worse, could have been Staten Island." I don't usually indulge in the time-honored borough-bashing so beloved of my fellow citizens, but I'd a grudge about Staten Island that wasn't going away any time soon.

Danny had Captain Tal cruise along the coastline, just outside the markers that showed where they shouldn't go, until Ellen could say for certain where the trail led, and he marked it on a map he'd pulled out of his jacket pocket. Then Danny nodded at Tal, and the *Mercy Me* headed back to the Basin, where the captain saw them off with an invitation to hire her any time again. Apparently, having someone spend most of the day throwing up in a bucket wasn't enough to put her off, so long as they paid in cash.

The investigator still looked a little green, and he was staggering rather than swaggering as they walked down the pier, but Ellen wasn't going to point out any of that. The sway of the boat had actually felt a lot like current, the outsides finally matching the way she felt inside during a thunderstorm, or when Genevieve had her try to draw down current from a man-made source and then reshape it to her own needs.

She wasn't going to say any of that, either. But she held the knowledge to herself, that this was a thing she could do. It was a small thing, probably a stupid thing, but it was *hers.*

"So what now?" The more she focused on the connection, the more the need to find those three teenagers chewed at her. Now that they had an idea where to go, she wanted to go *now.*

"The fact that you were able to pinpoint them probably means that they're still alive," Danny said. "And the fact that they're still alive means that whoever has them intends to keep them around for a while longer."

Ellen listened to what he was saying, and thought that she heard something else, underneath.

"But what do they want them for?" she asked. "And..." And what is being done to them? She didn't ask that, either. She knew enough to know that it probably wasn't good.

Danny sighed, and shook his head, removing the baseball cap and wiping his arm across his forehead, to clear away the sweat. His curls were sea- and sweat-damp, the fine lines around his eyes more visible now than they'd been under direct sunlight. If you could ignore the horns more visible through his damp curls, he looked a hundred percent human, and really tired.

"I want to look at a better map, see if I can pinpoint exactly where you were targeting, and also figure out the best way to get there. I don't suppose you drive?"

Ellen blinked. "Of course I do."

That got a laugh out of him. "Right. Suburban girl, right?"

"City boy", making it sound like an insult. The words slipped out of her mouth, and she almost didn't realize they'd come from her. She knew—she *knew*—he wasn't going to yell at her for sass, or get pissed off, but her breath still hitched for a second, her body bracing itself.

"I can drive," he said, mildly. "Only last time I did, it was a patrol car, and my instincts are not what you want out among civilians."

She was diverted, trying to imagine him in a uniform. "Did you ever do a high speed chase?"

"Never once. But I do occasionally forget to stop for red lights. Or stop signs. It's safer just to not let me behind the wheel."

"I don't have a job, to rent a car, though." Ellen felt she should make a clean breast of everything. "I don't even have a bank account, or a cable bill, or anything. They ask you for all that, when you rent." She'd come to New York with a friend, who had rented their car, and she remembered the excess of paperwork that had been required.

"So I rent, and we put you down as a driver. You're staying with Valere?"

"No." She had slept on the couch for the first month, until Genevieve got her office cleared out. Now she had her own place, an off-the-books sublease, but it was so tiny, and she spent so little time there, she'd never gotten around to acquiring Stuff. Not that she had much; she'd left home with just her backpack, and living in the Park the way she'd done, you didn't keep much in the way of belongings. Even if you tried, they'd disappear pretty soon.

"Hrm." He made a noise she didn't understand, but then they

were on the street and he was raising his hand to hail a cab, and she didn't want to ask any more questions, while they were in public, even if it was only one cabbie listening in.

"How urgent does it feel?" he asked, out of the silence. Ellen was taken aback suddenly—she'd slipped easily into follow-the-lead, and wasn't expecting to be put on the spot again.

"Urgent," she said. She didn't know what not-urgent felt like; the people she Saw were about to get dead, so urgent was the only way she knew to feel. Then she thought about it a little more. When she'd Seen Genevieve and the guy who had died, Stosser, it had felt urgent, too. But nothing had happened for a couple of days after, and Genevieve hadn't died at all, because... because something had changed. Because she had changed something, by telling them.

So. Urgent, yes. Death was always urgent. But maybe they had time.

"They're not dead yet." She was pretty sure about that, especially after what Danny had said. Pretty sure, but not absolutely. She licked her lips, trying not to think about the cabbie who might or might not be eavesdropping. She tried not to think about her mother, who had told her all these things she said she saw meant that she was crazy, or lying. She tried not to think about anything, except the sense of three figures, ghostly but real, lingering in her brain.

No, not her brain. Genevieve had explained that. Her core. The place where current coiled inside, the magic everyone had access to, but only Talent could handle, channel, and manipulate. Only Talent, like her, could hold inside.

She was a Storm-Seer. She Saw things in the current that even other Talent couldn't. She saw Death, and the dying. She wasn't crazy, she wasn't lying, and Danny needed her in order to find them.

Had Genevieve felt different, after the other one, Stosser, had died? Yes. A subtle, slight difference, like feeling silk under your hand instead of silky cotton, but there. Maybe. If that's what the difference was.

She needed more visions to learn what they meant, but she never wanted to have another vision, ever.

"Can you feel anything more than that?" He was pushing, but he wasn't pushing *her*, he was pushing for *them*. That made it okay.

"Hurt. Weak. Angry. Afraid. Angry most of all." That was what had reached her, their anger and fear; they did not want to die.

"At risk?"

She thought, reaching mental hands down the way Genevieve had taught her, stroking the waves of current in her core, letting the ripples run over invisible fingers until the knowledge reached her brain.

"Yes."

"Do you need to get anything from your apartment?"

He was taking her with him. He'd promised, and yet the confirmation was equal parts relief and fear. Relief, because she needed to do this, needed to see it through, to know that yes, she had helped, that it wasn't just chance, that there was a *reason* that she Saw all this. And fear because... well, she might be crazy but she wasn't stupid.

"No." She'd spent days in the same clothes, before. She could buy a toothbrush and a comb, if needed, and they weren't about to go hungry. Everything else was just details.

"Right. I need to get a few things from the office, and," he checked his watch, "yeah, there's enough time to swing by and rent a car."

Ellen decided not to tell him that the *Mission: Impossible* theme just started playing in her head.

47

When we got back to the office, I sent Ellen off to pick up some road trip essentials—water, soda, sandwiches, and a stack of whatever daily newspapers were still on the stands. We could have picked all that up once we were out of the city, but there was something I needed to do that required her being out of earshot.

But the voice that picked up on the other end of the line was male, not female.

"Exactly how fucked up is she?"

To give Didier credit, he didn't hesitate, or ask what I was talking about, or who.

"We don't know. Bad, but not broken."

"If I'd thought she was broken I wouldn't have let her stick around," I said impatiently. Jesus, did they think I was an idiot, or that masochistic?

"A purely clinical assessment?" Sergei went on. "She's got some serious self-worth issues, probably inevitable from second-guessing her sanity for the past ten years, once her Talent kicked in and nobody told her what was happening. She then fell in with a group that first told her she was special and then rejected her, and was then informed that she was not only not-crazy, but she had a skillset that was going to direct her life for, well, the rest of her life. Within those parameters, she's not fucked up at all."

"Within those parameters." Like saying a cobra wasn't dangerous, within the parameters of it being able to kill you with one shot if you disturbed it, and oh guess what, you won't see it until you step on it.

"Is there a problem?"

"No." I was used to working with high-res Talent, and poking at temperamental fatae, and going toe-to-toe with the least-appealing of humanity. Relatively speaking, this was a piece of cake. "I just wanted to know where the stress lines were."

"So we shouldn't expect her home tonight?"

48

And damned if Didier didn't have the Big Bad Daddy voice down perfect. I almost felt guilty.

"I need her to keep me on track, to find these kids." I could do it myself, but it would take longer. And, I'd promised her.

"If she can help you, it will help her."

"Yeah."

"Tell her to ping Wren if anything, and I mean *anything* goes to hell."

I blinked, and cursed myself for an idiot. Just because I couldn't use the ping, and neither could a human like Didier, that was no reason to ignore a damned useful tool.

"I'll do that."

The external door to the office opened, and I reached across my desk for the box I'd pulled out of the lower drawer, before Didier had answered the phone. "Gotta go. Give the little woman my best," I said, and hung up before Didier finished laughing.

"Danny?"

She came into the inner sanctum's doorway, but didn't pass the threshold. She wasn't carrying anything, so I assumed that she'd put the bags down already.

"Checking in with another client," I said, lying smoothly. If her self-esteem issues were as serious as it seemed, then the idea that I was checking in with her mentor—okay, her mentor's significant other—wouldn't help any, no matter how normal a thing it was.

Normal if she were a normal teenaged Talent, I reminded myself. She wasn't normal, and she wasn't a teenager. I was painfully aware of both facts just then, as she leaned against the doorframe, for once not over-conscious of herself, and watched me.

She was a long drink of water, strong-shouldered and nicely tapered, and when she stopped worrying about other people noticing her, she had a regal sort of grace that matched her face. She was young, yeah, but in no way shape or form a child.

49

Fortunately, I was older and had learned how to put a lockdown on my libido before she was even born. No matter her age, she was damaged; the usual flirt-work pattern I had with Bonnie was not the way to go here.

"Car's reserved. There's a toiletries kit in the bathroom, under the sink. Grab it and let's go." I opened the box in my hand, and took out the extra case of bullets. I hadn't needed to shoot at anything other than a target in years, but I never assumed that was going to be the situation going forward.

"She's doing what?" Wren Valere put down the set of locks she had been playing with, and looked incredulously at her partner. "She was supposed to tell him what she Saw, and then come home, not run off playing Private Eye."

Sergei didn't disagree with her, but Hendrickson had been telling him what was going down, not asking permission. "Danny said that she was helping him track down the missing teens, something about her vision maintaining a thread?"

"Huh." Wren considered that. "A variant on a signature, maybe?" She wasn't all that interested in the hows of current, just so long as she could make it work. "Okay, I can see that, and why he'd take full advantage. No dummy, our Danny. But—" She bit down on what she was going to say. "No, I'm overreacting. Danny's a perfectly responsible adult, most of the time, and he won't let her get into trouble. And it's good that she get a first-hand look at the fatae community, right?"

"Right."

Sergei didn't quite trust her calm. His partner, normally unflappable, had been decidedly flapped ever since she accepted the mentorship of a half-grown, totally untrained Talent, and this should have sent her into a small panic, not calmed her down.

"And he'll be able to take care of her. Unless they run into another Talent. If they do, she's helpless. She barely knows how to maintain her own core, she's barely at first-level cantrips, and if she gets hit with another vision? She's a sitting target when that happens."

Wren Valere took a shallow breath, and leaned back against the sofa, staring out at the brilliant view out her apartment windows. Sergei waited.

"I'm doing that thing where you roll your eyes and tell me every mentor in the entire history of mentoring has had the exact same doubts and panics."

"You are."

"And Ellen's smart, and reasonably savvy, and oh by the way not an idiot teenager amuck with hormones and the need to show off."

"Exactly."

"And the best way for her to stop being afraid of her visions is to see, first-hand, that they can be used in a proactive way, too. That she's not helpless, she's actually incredibly powerful."

She knew that already: Ellen had been part of the circle that caught a serial killer team. Admittedly, Bonnie and the other PUPs had been in control but it was Ellen's storm-seer sense that had allowed them to harness the storm.

"And if she really needs help, she will ping for it." Wren frowned. "She will, won't she? She won't go all stubborn and independent and decide she can handle it herself?"

"What, you mean like you would?" Sergei's lips twitched as she glared at him. "No, I don't think so. Even if she hadn't seen how well Bonnie and her crew work together, Danny won't let her."

But inwardly, shoved far below even the levels his partner could read, Sergei wasn't so sure. Ellen had something she needed to prove, even if she wasn't vocalizing that need yet. And, he knew all too well, a Talent with something to prove...sometimes took stupid risks.

5

Once Ellen had identified our probable destination, I'd started working on a plan. Like most plans, it depended on a dollop of luck, a smidge of skill, and the smile of the gods. But then, that was pretty much the MO of the boardwalk, any given night.

My shadow, apparently, had never been down the Shore.

"Wow." Ellen had a strange look on her face, like she wanted to grin, but was afraid it would be impolite. "It really is…. It really *is.*"

I looked around, trying to see it through her eyes. "Yeah, it really is." The boardwalk was transitioning between day and night, some sunbathers still sprawled out on the sand even as the workers in the game booths began their calls, to win a prize and impress your girl. I could remember coming here as a teenager, and it had seemed exactly the same, back then. Even the people seemed the same: the teenagers in packs, the families with a small child wide-eyed and babbling with excitement, the occasional senior citizens walking slowly, and every now and again the bright "beep beep beep" of an electric cart bringing people from one end of the boardwalk to the other, almost but never quite running someone over. The booths were garish and overly-bright, the darkness hanging over the ocean somehow comforting and threatening all at once, the sound of the cold Atlantic surf a scarce murmur under the many voices.

I'd worked one of those booths as a teenager, lived in a house off the beach with seven other guys, worked all night, slept most of the day, not worried about anything except saving enough of my paycheck that my mother didn't kill me at the end of the summer. Hadn't been back, since.

This wasn't a vacation. The clock was ticking, a metronome in the back of my head, driving me on. Lives at risk, and I was the only one looking.

"How are we going to find anyone, or anything here?" Ellen asked. "It's a zoo."

"Ask a zookeeper," I said.

Ellen had to show I.D. at the bar, which was a difference from when I'd been down here, but the inside of Doblosky's was what I'd been expecting: bare wood walls and benches, a long bar that would be three-deep by midnight, and bartenders who already looked tired. We moved up to the bar, and I leaned against it, removing the baseball cap and ruffling the sweat-damp hair so that my horns didn't show through. Ellen leaned in at my side, not too close but clearly with me.

The bartender took a professional look, the kind that didn't see anything but remembered everything in case it was needed later. "What can I get you folks?"

"Yuengling, draft."

"Two," Ellen said. I was pretty sure she wasn't a drinker, but Yuengling was a good basic lager: decent enough to not get you sneered at, common enough that nobody would think you were trying too hard. And if she left it half-drunk it wasn't going to break the budget.

The bartender nodded once. "PI?"

I spread my hands, fair-caught. "After a while, it starts to show." Actually, it didn't, not on my face. The bartender was good, and experienced—he might even have been here twenty years ago when I did my time. "I bet you get a lot of that down here."

The guy shrugged. He had hands like baseball gloves, and a torso to match, but his face was more like a college professor's: narrow, with dark hair slicked back, and thoughtful eyes.

"Missing kids, mostly. Sometimes a missing spouse."

"Kids. Late teens. Two girls and a boy."

"Runaways?"

"Maybe. Probably not."

The bartender finished pulling our beers and set them down in front of us, hearing what I wasn't saying. "This ain't back when. Not much like that going down here."

"Not much isn't none."

Ellen stirred next to me, but only reached out to pick up her beer, and take a sip. I wondered what she'd been about to say, and why she'd stopped herself.

The bartender went down the line, dealing with other customers, and Ellen let out a little sigh.

"What?"

"How do you know what to say? How do you know if something's too much to tell them?"

"Experience." That probably wasn't what she wanted to hear, but it was all I had.

"If it was just boys, I might have something for you," the bartender said, coming back like the conversation'd never been interrupted. "House downtown is the place for that, lost boys end up there. But girls aren't their thing and the cops are watching too close for anything else to go on right now."

I looked sideways at Ellen, who was staring down into her beer

54

like answers to a test she hadn't studied for were written in the foam. Anyone would have thought the faint shake of her head was her reaction to the taste. I wasn't anyone.

"They're together, last we heard," I said. "So yeah, probably not our scene." I made note of it, though. Prostitution was, my way of thinking, a valid lifestyle choice—hell, I sold my physical skill and a breed of comfort too, if you wanted brass tacks—but only if the people involved were of legal age and consent. A few unofficial pokes into the house's business would determine if official notice should be taken. I'd been a city cop, not Jersey, and I'd never worked Vice, but I still knew who to call.

"Nothing else floating under the surface?" I paid for our drinks, an additional two twenties folded into the tab.

"The usual graft and corruption, but it's been under control for a couple-three years by now. Bad business to let anything else in. You know how it is."

Yeah, I knew. The casinos had taught everyone else how to keep their backyards clean, the better to rake money in through the front door. If you kept under their radar you could survive, but pop up once....

"Thanks."

"Good luck," the bartender said, and one of my twenties came back to me, along with a handful of dimes in change. "I got teenagers, myself."

I nodded, and drank my beer.

"So what now?" Ellen had gotten halfway through hers, and then pushed it away, reaching instead for the bowl of bar-mix. "Got more bartenders to hit up, or are we going to pile back into the car and drive around randomly until we find them?"

My shadow had claws. Tiny milk-claws, but claws. That was good to know.

"We could do a survey of all the bars," I said. If the missing kids

55

had been human, that's what I would have done. But what she'd Seen changed that plan. "But no to both of your questions." I'd stopped here to eliminate possibilities. Now it was time to open them up again.

Unfortunately, I'd have to wait until full dark for that. Some of the fatae could wander the beaches and boardwalks without being noticed—all right, some of us in bathing suits would probably make people do a doubletake or three—but the one in particular I needed to question raised a massive fuss every time, and I was in no mood for fuss. So there was some time to kill.

We stopped outside the bar to pick up dinner—a hot dog for Ellen, two slices of cheese pizza for me—and an extra pastrami sandwich, hold the slaw and mustard. The guy gave me a doubting look, but made the sandwich anyway.

"For later?" Ellen asked, as we walked away, heading not down the boardwalk but toward the nearest ladder down to the beach itself.

"For bribes."

The sand was almost too soft to walk on, courtesy of all the sunbathers, but we took off our shoes and slogged toward the water, a dark glint in the distance. I could see the city's lights, and something that was probably Staten Island, plus a couple of larger ships out beyond the markers. And, off to the side, the movement of something sliding through the water, then disappearing again.

I decided not to mention the shark to Ellen. It wasn't like we were going to go in all that deep. Just enough to be polite.

I took the sandwich out of the waxed paper bag, and peeled off the bread, shoving it back in the bag—no use wasting good rye, after all.

"What are you doing, going fishing?" She wasn't being snarky: she really had no idea. Valere had been slacking on this side of her education.

56

"Not exactly. But kind of. Stay here."

I left her ankle-deep in the surf, and moved forward, holding the meat in my left hand. With my luck I'd end up either getting nibbled at by a shark, or hit on by an inquisitive fendha. Neither of those would be useful, right now. Or, actually, ever.

"I'm looking for information," I said, trusting the night air and ebbing tide to carry my words. "No tricks, no traps. Looking for information on a trace carried in these waters, from Manhattan to here. Three traces, unhappy or angry or scared."

No answer. I didn't want to influence the witnesses—you never gave them any info they could build off, so nobody could say you led them—but a little glide for the ride could be overlooked. I shook the meat gently, letting the smell of it carry on the night air. "I'm offering dinner, to seal the trade."

There was no response, although I could hear something slapping the surface a few meters out. Unlike in the city, when I could play on my rep, I had to be more cautious here. This wasn't my turf, and the politics of who answered to whom could tangle me up badly, if I wasn't careful.

Still. Not as bad as the time I had to go to Denver.

"Nobody out there knows anything? I guess the Shore's reputation is oversold, then."

When in doubt, insult the fatae. It's not advice I'd give to humans, but I've found it remarkably effective over the years.

A louder slap on the water, and then something moved under the dark waves, a too-large mass coming too fast at me.

I held my ground. Sand. Whatever.

The mass stopped just shy of ramming into me, and a darker, more solid shape rose from the waves. The head was the size of a football, and shaped about the same, with a neck that managed to be both muscular and sinewy at the same time. The shadow underneath suggested that a more massive body was attached to

57

that neck, but I wasn't going to poke it to find out.

"Yes." The voice was high, but masculine. As far as you could make assumptions about that sort of thing, anyway.

"Yes, what? Yes you have information, or yes, nobody knows anything?"

"We know."

I had no idea what breed this kid was, but it was clearly a groupthink type. Or maybe kid here was a split personality. So long as one of them had the info to share, I didn't give a fuck.

We stared at each other for a bit—or I stared, and it waited. If it had eyes, they weren't immediately obvious, just long whiskers dripping from either side of the football, the entire thing covered in gleaming black scales. Even its mouth was a narrow slit, the jaw dropping when it talked, but no teeth visible.

That didn't mean this thing wasn't dangerous, though.

"You want?" I held up the meat carefully, trying not to give any invitation for it to snap it out of my hand—and maybe take my hand along with it.

The head lowered slightly, and it took the meat from me like a cat tasting treats, soft and steady. One second the chunk of corned beef was in its mouth, hanging over the side, and the next it was gone, swallowed whole like…well, like a snake would snork down a mouse. I guess the analogy made sense, all structural resemblance considered.

It wavered back and forth in front of me like a damned sea-cobra, either digesting or getting ready to strike, and then it said, "Five night ago. We heard them screaming."

I tensed: screaming was never good. But "heard" was open to interpretation, especially coming from a breed that didn't seem to have ears. "A little more detail than that, please?"

"We were feeding. Over us, a ship. Not-large, not a barge, but larger than the usual ones that come here."

This was a public beach; anything larger than a two-person sailboat would probably get waved off by the lifeguards, assuming they didn't get grounded on a sandbar. But if this was late at night, there would be no lifeguards, and if they came in at high tide...

"And you heard screaming."

The serpent stared at me.

"Were those screaming on the deck, or-?"

"From inside. We heard them, as they passed over"

Vibrations. Of course. I'd save feeling dumb for later.

"The water shivered with their fear. We followed, as far as we dared, but there were too many humans. Too much light and noise, when they come to shore."

"Thank you," I said. "I am sorry the meal was so small."

The serpent stilled, like I'd insulted it, or it had no idea what the hell I'd said, and then it slid back into the water, barely a ripple marking its passing, and the dark shadow writhed and roiled back into the depths.

That hadn't been its body, I realized: that had been its entire school. I'd been surrounded. Jesus fucking Christ.

I turned around and sloshed back to shore, picking up Ellen along the way.

"Was that...another fatae?"

"Yeah."

"What kind?"

"I have no idea. The sea-going breeds are kinda standoffish. Swimoffish. Finoffish? They don't come hang out with landfolk often."

"But it had something useful?"

"Yeah." I didn't know how much to tell her. I wasn't used to working with a partner—the times I'd done work for PUPI, I still worked it on my own, and reported back, mostly, and NYPD protocol was laughably useless here.

59

"Five nights ago, a boat came in, unloaded bodies that might or might not be our kids. I'm guessing they are, since there's no reason fatae would be interested in ordinary humans being hauled out."

"And?"

She was looking at me so expectantly, the lights from the boardwalk catching the turn of her head, the cant of her body, that I felt like not being able to say "So here's what we're going to do," was an utter and absolute failure of myself as a human being.

Since I'm not entirely human, this didn't bother me as much as it should have.

But it still bothered me.

"And...I don't know," I admitted. "'A boat' is too vague, and it's not like there are eyes on the beach we can hack. I'd been hoping they knew something more specific. Right now, the trail ends here. Unless we pick up something new, or you suddenly get a flash of something..."

The clock ticks on every missing kid case. These were older teenagers, and there were three of them, together, so the clock would slow down a little, but every day that went by, the damage risks went up until the difference between retrieval and failure was not much difference at all.

I didn't say any of that out loud, but I'd figured that Shadow was pretty good at reading the silence.

"They're going to die. I only see people if they're going to die."

"Valere didn't die." I put my hand on her arm, not curling my fingers around, just resting them on her skin. If she wanted to move away, she could, no resistance. "Wren Valere is alive, and well. You see a possible future. Yeah, it's the most possible, the most probable. But nothing's set in stone. Nothing's foreordained. You know Bonnie, I'm sure she's talked to you about kenning."

"Yeah." She didn't pull away, didn't move. She didn't sound convinced, either.

"Bonnie sees the highest likelihood of events coming together. But even one push can bring it all down, or send it in a different direction. Bonnie's like…like a shove. You're a battering ram. Just your Seeing has the potential to change things."

I sounded smooth, persuasive, convincing. Fact was, I didn't have fucking clue how much impact she had, although what I'd said about Bonnie was truth, far as Bonnie had explained it to me. But what mattered was that Shadow bought it.

"You're full of shit."

I probably shouldn't have laughed, but I couldn't help it. She wasn't mad, she wasn't offended, she was just so matter of fact, it was funny.

"I am. But I really do believe that the fact that you started people looking, started *me* looking, that we're asking questions, has the potential to change things."

"Change it enough?"

I sighed, and let my hand drop from her arm as we started walking again toward the lights and noise of the Boardwalk. "That, yeah. That's the question, isn't it?"

"So…we keep looking," she said.

Yeah. We kept looking.

6

Danny was used to working alone. Ellen had known that, figured that she'd be a tagalong, useful for... well, she didn't know what she would be useful for, actually. But she wasn't going to be left behind, to sit and stress and not know what was going on. Not this time.

And, unlike Genevieve, and even Bonnie and the other Pups, Danny Hendrickson didn't seem to think that she needed to be sheltered and protected, or act like she was some kind of bomb that was going to go off if someone spoke too loudly, or said the wrong thing. She'd made a Hulk joke, once, and only Sergei got it, which was just sad.

If being a Talent meant giving up pop culture, Ellen wasn't sure she wanted any part of it. Except she didn't have a choice, apparently. This was the road she'd been put on, and she had no real choice but to walk it. So she would.

While she was shaking sand off her feet, Danny had cornered a bunch of teenagers by one of the hundred and seven pizza places that lined the boardwalk, and was asking them questions, showing them the sketch she had done of the three faces. The teenagers were shaking their heads: another dead end. Ellen considered them, and then considered how little the hot dog had done to fill her stomach, and let instinct and hunger lead her to a nearby pizza stand, a long counter facing the boardwalk, with tables and plastic chairs arranged in the back. It wasn't busy, so she leaned her elbows on the counter the way she'd seen Danny do in the bar and waited for someone to notice her.

The guy behind the counter was old, maybe in his forties, and looked like he should have been cast in a mob movie. But his eyes were tired, and kind.

"A slice and a Diet Coke, please."

"Pepsi okay?"

Ellen made a face, and the guy laughed. "How about a root beer?"

"That's good yeah, thanks." She pulled out her wallet, and counted the bills, then handed them to the guy as he shouted her order to the younger guy by the ovens, and handed her a drink. It was pre-made, and the ice was melting already, but the salty air and the walking and the beer almost two hours ago had left her thirsty enough to not care.

She turned to watch Danny, who had let the kids go, folding the sketch back into the inside pocket of his jacket.

"You work here long?" She turned back and asked the guy, as he slid her pizza across the counter, the grease already seeping through the two white paper plates underneath.

"Twenty-seven years this summer," he said proudly. "Family business, still."

"Nice. I bet you get a lot of regulars."

"Some. But there's always turnover. Kids, you know?" He said it like she wasn't barely five years older than some of the kids he was talking about—and some of them might even be older than she was. She felt older, though. A lot older.

"Three of my friends were down here, last week." She had no idea what she was doing, but she'd been watching Danny, and listening, and maybe it was time to be more than just a tagalong. "We were supposed to meet them, but… " She shrugged, tried to make it seem both important and no big deal. She'd been blown off before, dumped by people she thought were friends, who would have her back. She scooped up some of that bitterness, held it in her stomach, and let it blend with the worry she had for the three faces she had Seen in her vision. "If they took off and didn't tell me, I'm going to kill them."

The guy laughed, and leaned on the counter, mimicking her pose. "It's summer, it's the Shore. Stuff happens. You can't reach 'em on your cell?"

"It goes straight to voicemail. All three of them." She let a little more worry creep in. "You don't think anything bad happened to them, do you?"

"Bad things can happen," the guy said. "But no, I suspect you're right, they just flaked, and you can kick their asses all the rest of the year for it. But hey, hang on. Justin!"

The kid by the ovens turned, and she saw that he was younger than she'd thought, maybe sixteen at most. "Yeah?"

"C'mere," the guy said, and swung his arm. "This is my son, Justin. He notices faces better than I do, especially at that age. Maybe he saw 'em."

Ellen started, her mind suddenly going blank. "I—"

"Here," and Danny was next to her, his hand sliding the sketch across the counter. "Visuals help better—El's been known to forget what color her own eyes are, much less someone else's."

"Hey," she protested, and felt his arm reach around her waist, pulling her close. It should have felt awkward, but it didn't: she was reassured, and warmed in a way that had nothing to do with the air temperature, or the sweat already on her skin.

64

"You know it's true," Danny was saying. "Anyway, nobody's seen them, so if this is a dead end too, I think we're going to have to admit defeat."

The pizza guy had looked up at Danny, then back at her, and he looked like he was going to say something, and then shrugged. Ellen could guess—Danny wasn't that much older than her, maybe a decade?—but it was enough to raise a few eyebrows, the way Danny was playing it. Definitely not "older brother" style, or tagalong not-quite-partner.

"Nah," the kid, Justin, said. "I didn't see 'em. Sorry."

Out in the distance, over the water, there was a flash of heat-lightning, zigging from one cloud to the other, less a threat of rain than a reminder that it was still summer, that changeable forces still loomed overhead. Ellen didn't see the flash behind her; she didn't have to. She felt it, knew exactly where it was, how far away, how powerful, although she had no science training or instruments to measure it. She knew because the vision hit her like an icepick, bypassing her walls and digging right into the softest part of her brain.

Genevieve had taught her how to make it easier, how to let the visions in rather than having them knock her barriers over. It helped, a little: like diving into a tornado instead of being swept off your feet, she supposed, and then there wasn't any time to think, her mind sorting through what she Saw, trying to put it into some kind of order.

She felt Danny grab her arm, leading her away from the noise and bustle of the booths. Her body followed automatically, but the rest of her was inside a room filled with shadows. Her visions didn't have smell, and rarely sound—when they called it Sight they weren't kidding. So she *looked*, and the shadows became distinct shapes: boxes, and tables, mostly. She was in a storeroom of some kind.

65

Then one of the shadows moved, coming toward her, and there was a hand reaching out to her, pale and slender, palm turned up. There was webbing between the fingers, and something glittered faintly on the skin, even in the dim light.

Then the scene changed, wrenching Ellen along with it, and she was in the middle of a street, dark and abandoned. Rows of neat little houses sat along either side, with cars parked at the curb. She looked up, all the way down the street, her sight telescoping in a way that made her want to throw up, and she saw the beach, and the ocean. Too far away. Too far away to be safe.

"Safe from what, Ellen? Safe from what?"

She tried to walk toward it, but something had her by the ankles, and she couldn't move, couldn't step forward, only back, the weights pulling her back into the shadowed room, and she knew if she went back there she would never escape.

"Ellen?"

She made an irritable noise, and tried to flap her hand at him, to tell him to shut up. He must have taken the hint because he didn't say anything more, although he still had a hand on her arm, somewhere outside the vision.

The street was nice, the houses in decent repair, what she could see in the night. Was it tonight? She looked up, and checked the moon, hanging high in the black. Tonight, or close enough. Tonight or tomorrow. But where?

She needed more. Needed to see more.

Unable to move from where the vision had dropped her, she couldn't turn to see the cross-street, but it was narrow, almost like an alley, and had more houses on it, smaller ones, almost like cottages. Carlyle, she read off the nearest street sign, squinting to read the letters.

Not enough.

You're a storm-seer. Genevieve had explained it to her, the two of

66

them sitting on a bench in Central Park. The sky had been bright blue, the air clear and cool. Genevieve had said it was safer to talk about it then. *We all pull power from current, the magic that run along electricity, but you have an extra gift. Current carries things with it. Memories. Images. You can see them. You can pull them from the current, before they even happen.*

More current. She reached for the power she could feel racing overhead, riding along those lightning flashes out at sea. All those years of denying she saw anything, trying to fit in, it seemed almost wrong how easy it was to find the current, bring it in toward her...

Too much, too many conflicting sparks. She fell to her knees, the current prickling painfully up and down her spine, unable to settle, and the vision was lost.

"Ellen. Ellen, come on. Come with me. No, it's okay," and he was talking to someone else now, his voice pitched away from her, "She's ok, I think that last beer did her in."

She wanted to protest, but her knees felt like rubber and her head was burning and all she really wanted to do was lie down somewhere until the fireworks scrambling inside her settled down and behaved.

"You did something with current, didn't you? And it burned you. It's okay, you're going to be okay."

Yes. She knew that. She was the Talent here, not him, and she opened her mouth to say that, but all that came out was a harsh gasp.

"Come on, sit down." And she was being lowered onto a bench, and Danny was sitting next to her, his arm around her shoulders.

"I Saw," she said, barely a whisper. "I saw...her. One of the girls. She's alive, she'll be alive, but I don't know about the others." The last time she had seen someone twice, it had been Genevieve...and the one missing from that second vision had already died, although she hadn't known it at the time.

67

"And I saw… outside. Outside where she is." Although she didn't know for certain the cellar was on that street, why else would she be seeing it? "A street. Hamlin? No, Carlyle. Carlyle Court."

She felt him shift, reaching for something, and then he swore under his breath. "You scorched my cell." There was no condemnation in his voice, just resignation. "No way to get a new one before morning. But the street, it's near here?"

She nodded. "Yeah. Not here, the town's not like this one." The town they'd driven through had cottages the same size, but they were clearly rentals, more run-down, nowhere near as carefully tended. "I could see the beach from there, sort of. Down the end of the road. A private beach? Not like this."

"Beach town, nicer, Carlyle Court. Okay." His arm left her, and she opened her eyes to see him watching her intently, his face in shadows from the streetlamp hanging over them. "You okay?"

"Yeah." The current had settled, finally, and she no longer thought she was going to throw up. She didn't want to try standing up just yet, though.

"All right. Hang tight for a minute."

She wasn't sure what that meant, to hang tight, but she was all right with sitting there while he went off, approaching an older couple walking past them. They spoke for couple of minutes, and then Danny held up his phone as though showing it to them. The woman laughed, and the man nodded, and took out his own phone, entering something on the keyboard. They spoke a little more, and then Danny was coming back, his body language saying he had something, a direction, a scent to follow.

Oh yay. She forced herself to sit up straight, pretending that she was ready to go, not a burden at all.

Shadow looked even more like a shadow, like someone had

taken an eraser to her sharp edges. If I had an inch of compassion and any sense whatsoever, I'd throw her into the car and go back to the city, leave her there and come back tomorrow, alone.

I was pretty sure that her reaction to that wouldn't be pretty. And she'd be right. She was wrecked, but she'd been the one to see the missing kids, and she had a right to be in on it. If she wanted.

"Light Bay," I said.

She lifted her gaze enough to look at me. "What?"

"The only town around here that has a Hamlin Court, according to the Internet, is the town of Light Bay. It's about fifteen minutes north of here. You game?"

"Yeah. I… Yeah."

She wasn't. But she wasn't going to admit it, either.

"C'mon, tiger," I said, reaching out a hand. "Get to the car and you can sleep the rest of the way there."

I ended up half-carrying her the rest of the way. She'd gone silent and loose, like a little kid sullen with exhaustion, and only pride was keeping her upright. I didn't remember if this was normal for Talent—the ones I hung with tended to be, well, tougher than this.

"You okay?"

"Yeah." It was more of an exhale than an actual word, but she was buckling herself in, and her eyes were open. "Genevieve says that pulling wild current is harder than man-made, and the storm was pretty far away. I don't think I should have done it."

"So why did you?"

She shrugged, and looked out the passenger side window. "I don't… it's not like it is for everyone else. I don't always have a choice."

I started up the car and pulled out of the parking spot, careful to avoid the gaggle of drunk teenagers trying to cross the street in front of me. "The visions?"

69

"They come when they come. All I can do is…" and she waved a hand lazily in the air, "ride it."

She seemed to be waiting for me to say something. "That sucks."

Her laughter was bright, unforced, and an unexpected surprise, even if it didn't come with a smile. "Everyone else says I'm rare, or special. I spent my whole life wanting to be special. But yeah. It sucks."

7

Shadow fell asleep in the car. She slept like a little kid, her head lolling forward, snoring faintly. I kept the radio off, and drove through the night. I took route 35 up, rather than getting onto the Parkway, and had to focus on where I was going. Even so, my mind wouldn't let go of the case, and the echoes that every case invariably, inevitably, stirred.

Every case I take, when kids are involved, I hope to hell that they're runaways. Runaways, there's a reason they left. You can deal with reasons, whether it's getting them help, or getting them out of that situation and into a healthier one. You don't always get a happy-ever-after, but you get a better-for-now.

And most of my cases *are* runaways. Just not all of them.

This one could have been—three teenagers ditching a bad situation or boring relatives for something they hope will be better, in the relative wilds of the summer shore. Fatae teens were dumb as human ones. Even with Ellen seeing people in death's way, it could have been accident, or random chance…but it didn't feel like it.

These kids had been taken.

There were three reason why teenagers are abducted, as opposed to the myriad of reasons little kids are abducted. None of them were good. Some of them were worse. The fact that these kids were fatae didn't change any of that. In fact, an "exotic" would probably bring twice the money, for the discerning predator.

One, they were taken for the sex trade. Horrible as that sounded, it was almost the best option, because I could find them, then. And, assuming they didn't put up too much of a fight, they wouldn't be permanently damaged. Physically, anyway.

I had to unclench my fingers from the steering wheel when they started to hurt. Calling that the best option was only relative to the others. Option Two was that they'd been taken as slaves. The slave trade could be sexual or non-sexual, but there was less value, more turnover there… the moment a slave became trouble, they'd be killed. Three….

I'd never run into the third, but I knew about it. There was a small but very profitable market for victims. Disposable flesh, designed only to be hurt. When I was a cop, I'd seen the end result, fished out of basements, and buried in a closed casket.

Ellen had only seen one of the three in her most recent vision. The other two might have been asleep, or taken elsewhere. But they could also already be dead.

"There."

Ellen's voice was sleepy, but she was alert enough to catch the signpost I almost missed. Three quarters of a mile later, we were taking the exit for Light Bay.

"I don't suppose you have any sense of where to go?"

"It doesn't work that way. But it was residential, and near the beach. So away from downtown."

Such as downtown was, a single street of storefronts, all closed

72

and dark for the night already. This wasn't a hotspot. In fact, it was barely a warm spot on the map. I could imagine, in the daylight, it was cozy and quaint, the ideal place to take your pre-teens for a week down the shore, eat ice cream every afternoon and everyone's in bed by 10pm. The year-round locals were probably blue-collar, solidly working class of all races—probably a fair sprinkling of fatae, too. Two or three generations in one place, and the ones who leave probably come back, eventually, because once you've seen the rest of the world, this starts to look pretty good.

"This looks right," Ellen said, after I'd gone a few blocks east, driving slow enough to see but not so slow a late-patrolling cop would think to stop me. The local boys might be useful, but more likely we'd waste time and energy on territorial markings. "The houses look right."

They were seaside cottages, probably two bedrooms and a front parlor that could hold a pull-out bed, maybe another bedroom shoved into the attic. But they were all well kept-up, even in the moon and lamplight, the yards tended and the streets recently repaved. We drove along, and her attention scanned back and forth, not so much with her eyes but that weird blind look Talent got sometimes, the one that could seriously weird you out if you didn't know what they were doing.

I didn't plan it, but my right hand left the wheel, and reached out to touch her leg. Just a touch, my fingertips barely resting on the cloth, but it was enough to catch her attention. She looked down, smiled, just a corner of her mouth and a rise of her cheek, and then she went back to scanning.

"Anything?"

"It's not like a whatchamacallit, a GPS."

"You use a GPS?" The higher res a Talent, the less they were able to use tech. I'd thought that Shadow would be high res

73

enough to warrant a strict low-tech ruling—and her lack of training would make the situation even worse.

"My dad. At least now I know why it never worked properly when I was in the car." Her smile was gone, now. "He was right to blame me."

I'd already gotten the picture of her life before Bonnie and her crew dragged her in, but confirmation was always a kick in the gut. Bonnie said I had a white knight syndrome thing going, always wanting to rescue the helpless. She was only half right. I wanted to rescue *everyone*.

"Yeah, you guys are hell on electronics." There wasn't any point in candy-coating it: her parents hadn't been winners on the support front, but expecting them to know, or understand, what was happening…might as well ask a dog to do your taxes.

"They're gone."

"What?" I might have overreacted a little, because Ellen's hand covered mine suddenly, pressing down in reassurance. "Not gone-gone. Not here, gone. The feel of them's faded."

"Do you know where?"

She frowned, her eyes narrowing. "This would be easier if they were Talent," she said. "I think I've touched them enough, I'd be able to follow their signature."

I'd only ever heard the PUPs talk about signature, the feel of an individual's personal current. She'd learned that from Bonnie, not Wren.

"But you can't do that for fatae?"

"No, like I said, you feel …different. And this isn't signature, what I feel through the vision. It's… deeper, and softer, and…signature's something you follow. This is, it's leading me."

I wasn't Talent, I didn't give a damn about the technical aspects of current. From the look on Ellen's face, though, I suspected she was going to be cornering the PUPs, the *Cosa's* technicians, when she had a chance. "So they are fatae?" I was pretty damn sure, just based on her sketches, and the fact that the serpents had bothered to hear them, but…

"They feel… human but not. And the gills? So, yeah. Close enough to pass…"

"Like me?" We were still cruising the streets, although with less direction now. I came to the end of one road, facing the low seawall that kept the shore from the city, and pulled the car over to the curb. "What do I feel like, to you?"

It was a stupid question. I didn't even know why I was asking, or what she was going to say.

"Wood and wine, and a warm dirt road."

Okay, I absolutely hadn't expected that. From the look on her face, neither had she. I rolled the words around in my thoughts, and laughed. "Yeah, close enough. My genetic donor was a faun, so that makes sense. I–"

She wasn't listening. She'd gone glassy-eyed again, her fingers convulsing around my hand, her body bending over tense as a bowstring. Even I could feel the current crackling over her, even as I heard the book of heat-thunder in the distance out over the ocean.

"Ellen?" I didn't know what to do, if I should hold onto her, or pull away, or talk to her… my instinct was to protect her, to shield her from whatever was slamming into her so hard, and I couldn't, all I could do was sit there and watch.

I'm not good with being helpless. Never have been, that's why I ended up a cop in the first place.

"Danny. Danny, no."

She wasn't talking to me. Or, she wasn't talking to the me who was in the car. I unhooked my seatbelt and turned sideways, ignoring all doubt to yank her into my arms, holding her the way you would someone just yanked off a ledge, arms curved around her, keeping her steady without actually holding her down. One of the few things we learned in the academy that was actually useful on the street. That, and learning how to duck, mainly.

Slowly, her breath came back to normal, and she pushed away, a gentle request to back the hell off. I let go, but stayed alert.

"I saw you. Alone this time. At a...carnival? There were lights, booth lights, like the Boardwalk but it was...grubbier, and daylight. And banners flying and.. a gun."

"The other three?" I kept my voice soft and low, like I used to coax kids out of hiding places. Me and a gun, well, it wouldn't be the first time.

"I didn't see them. Only you."

"So we have no reason to believe that anything has changed. They're still alive," I said, although truthfully this could be taken either way. But hope keeps us moving, and she looked like she needed to move. "Let's go."

8

In the end, finding a carnival somewhere near Light Bay was easy. Danny pulled into a diner, they slid into a booth, and he asked the waitress. Between the menu being handed over, and Danny's second cup of coffee, they had not only directions, but gossip about how long the carnival had been coming around, who they probably had to pay off to keep those rides going, and how many times the local church had tried, and failed, to get them shut down for moral offenses, etcetera.

"Seriously?" Ellen's eyes were wide in a combination of awe and too-much-information as the waitress, finally, left them to their coffee in peace.

Danny nodded. "Seriously. People, mostly, want to tell you things. If someone doesn't want to talk, they're scared. Take the toughest, most morose bastard on the face of the earth, and give him a platform, and he'll talk for hours. They might not answer your questions, but they'll let enough slip that you can draw conclusions."

Despite the hour, the seriousness of everything, and her utter exhaustion, Ellen felt for the first time like they had a chance.

"Drink your coffee," he said, letting his lips curl in just the hint of a smile, suggesting that he felt the same way. "We have our destination."

At night, the fairgrounds were near-magical to little kids and love-struck couples. During the day, before the lights came up, it was probably borderline seedy, worn and workmanlike. This early in the morning, with dew glittering on the grass and canvas tents, the sun just barely lighting the sky, dark purple streaks fading away to pale blue, it had an unexpected, calm beauty.

"I used to love county fairs when I was a little kid," Ellen said. "We'd go once a year, morning to midnight, and we got to run wild. Ate such disgusting things…"

"I'll buy you a deep fried something," Danny said.

"Yeah, thanks anyway." She couldn't quite work up a real smile, not with the vision of him, and the gun, and the sensation of death still creeping around in her head, but she did appreciate the effort. "I suppose we…what? Go knock on the door?"

"You already did."

She yelped a little, jumping back as two men appeared in front of them. One of them was lean and long, the other low and square, like they'd been designed to be a salt and pepper set. The lean one was covered in a soft grey fur, like a pelt, and had a feline face. The squat one was softer, like a beanbag chair with feet.

"So you're here, and you have our attention. What do you want?" The *human* was silent in their question, but the way they were looking at them said it, pretty loud.

"My name's Daniel Hendrickson," Danny said, taking off his baseball cap and running his hand though his hair. It could have been the mark of nerves, if you weren't paying attention. Or, if you were, it would highlight the horns showing through the curls,

78

shutting down the accusation of human in their tone.

Ellen tried to shrink in on herself, calling on years of staying invisible, unseen, unnoticed. She wasn't a Retriever, though; it only worked when people wanted to discount and ignore her.

"Yeah, so?"

"I'm a private investigator," Danny went on, lifting his right hand to indicate he wasn't making a threat, while he reached into his back pocket and pulled out a little fold-over wallet, opening it one-handed to show the laminated card tucked inside.

"Yeah, so?" the fatae repeated, unimpressed without even looking.

"So you can either help a cousin out, quietly, or I can walk away and come back with a lot of official paperwork that will make your life more difficult than it has to be," Danny said, matching him tone for bored tone. He wasn't threatening, exactly, Ellen thought. He was...*promising*. Not bravado: a fact, backed by confidence. She wanted that, she wanted to learn how to do that so badly it made her teeth hurt.

Danny tilted his head a little to the left, and almost-smiled at the two figures blocking them. "And we both know that even a hint of red tape is going to screw your day a lot worse than answering a few uncomfortable questions."

"We'll take that chance," the second fatae said, finally speaking up. "Town and us have an understanding."

In other words, they'd paid off enough people that they weren't worried. Ellen might not be a trained PI but she knew enough to understand that. Danny could try to force the issue, but even if they could get backing from the cops, it would be at least a day and she didn't know what would happen to the kids then; the tension she'd felt during each vision, the knowledge that death was sliding its fingers around them, just waiting for the right moment to yank them into its domain.

79

The thought shivered in her core, and there was an odd echo of that shiver on the soles of her feet. Frowning, Ellen glanced down. They were standing on ordinary dirt, hard-packed and worn from a summer of foot traffic. Using the sense Genevieve had taught her, Ellen clicked over into mage-sight and tried to look again.

Ordinary dirt…but deep below, there was something that pulsed, a thick shimmering rope twisting like a slow heartbeat, running under her feet and off into the distance.

A ley line. Current ran with electricity, both man-made and natural. Most Talent looked in the air, but it was under their feet, too.

She pulled a strand of current from her core, letting the dark blue thread curl around her mental finger, and then sent it down the way she'd learned, letting the leading end touch the ley line.

It was a different energy than what she felt when a storm touched her: thicker, less a jolt than a shove. It felt… like Danny, she realized suddenly. Solid, steady, and weirdly calm for something that was inherently unstable. Storm-current was harsh, unpredictable, as likely to burn your core as fill it, if you weren't careful. This… ley lines were easy enough to find, but harder to draw on, Genevieve had said; harder, and less powerful, diluted through the earth the way they were. That was why most Talent didn't bother using them. The power flowed through it, Ellen could *feel* it. Only, rather than forcing power into her the way air-current did, the flow enticed her in, surrounded her, soaking down into her core like rain.

Her visions, unlike most other usage, didn't drain her core because they came in from outside, an external force. Still, the sensation of topping off the tank was like an endorphin kick, making her feel competent and capable, too… or at least able to bullshit others into thinking that she was.

Five seconds, that had taken her. But in five seconds, things had gone from casual to tense.

"So why don't you both get back into your car, and drive back somewhere safer?" the squat fatae said, and it didn't sound like a suggestion. "This is our space, and we don't want you in it. *Cousin.*" He smiled, showing teeth like a shark's, and the lean fatae next to him took a step forward, bring a knife up out of nowhere. He held it casually, but Ellen had no doubt that it could become a threat as easily as it had appeared.

For an instant, she thought about using some of the cantrips that Genevieve had taught her, maybe to call fire, or levitate something. But she couldn't think she had enough control to do more than piss the two fatae off, and maybe making things worse. But she needed to do something: the thought that the missing kids might be here, and they were going to be turned away, was too much for her to bear.

Something inside her core clicked and turned, the ley-current sliding into place and her eyes glazed over even as she stepped forward, in front of Danny, and placed her left hand, palm out, on the chest of the first fatae.

It took a lifetime to sort through the possibilities rushing at her, instinctively not looking too closely at anything but waiting until that right moment in time came to her.

"Cancer," she said. "It's already in you, moving through your body. Nasty."

Before he had time to react, she turned to the other. He tried to evade her, and her hand closed on his shoulder, instead. "Car wreck. Drunk. You won't die immediately though."

She let go, not wanting to keep the vision any longer than needed, and stepped back, blinking at them. They both looked like frogs, mouths open and eyes blinking.

"You want to know what else she can find out about you?"

81

Danny asked, and that soft voice didn't disguise any of the menace underneath, this time. "No, I don't think so. Why don't you just let us in, walk around, ask a few questions…and nothing has to get ugly."

Ellen breathed in and out, letting the current surge through her. Ordinary humans—Nulls—couldn't actually see current, but even though the fatae didn't use, it they could still sense it. That was what she'd been told, anyway, and from the way Tall and Squat were backing up, she was willing to believe it.

Nobody had ever been scared of her before, not even when they thought she was crazy. It didn't feel as good as she'd thought it would.

"Anyone complains about you, out you go," Squat said, like he was trying to regain ground.

"We will be as polite as your granny," Danny said. "Thank you, gentlemen. Have a lovely day."

The thugs backed off to what seemed like a safe distance, and they walked through the gates, and onto the carnival grounds proper. Ellen felt the ley line fade as they moved away, and pushed the last lingering bits of current back into her core. The tingling in her skin faded, and she made an involuntary but heartfelt noise that sounded a lot like "ugh."

"I don't know what the hell you did back there, but you did good," he said.

"I don't know what I did back there either," she admitted. "Can I not have to do it again?"

Danny wasn't a Talent. He couldn't understand—it wasn't just that the visions were painful, or that she was tired of death aiming for her like cupid with his bow—she was a Storm-Seer, according to everyone, and it was like being an epileptic or color blind or something, just a thing you dealt with and adapted for and she got that she really did, but-

"I don't want to know that much about other people. I don't want to know what's going to happen to them. It's too much." She could *still* see it in her head, even though she'd tried not to look, tried not to notice anything, but it was all there. Death called the most strongly, limned itself with fire and frost, but every end result of every act and inaction was still there, hanging in the current around everyone.

And then Danny's hand was on her arm, curved around the crook of her elbow, and the fire dampened, the frost melted, and all Ellen felt was tired.

"Come on, Shadow," he said. "Time to be eye candy while I do some work."

That was just ridiculous enough to make her laugh.

My quip had covered up hell of a lot of uncertainty. I wasn't quite sure what the hell had happened back there at the gate: everything I'd ever heard of Storm-Seers, which admittedly wasn't a hell of a lot except what Bonnie had told me after Ellen showed up on the scene, said that they were only able to read the future randomly, when the current spikes were strong enough, and never in a particularly directed manner, the way she just had, by touching them.

I had a passing thought that maybe she'd made it up—I mean, who the hell would know—but I knew the signs of current-exhaustion well enough. Whatever had gone on, it had drained her significantly. And she looked unhappy enough for it to be real. There were folk who could fake me out, but Shadow wasn't anywhere in their league.

The sun had finally gotten up high enough that the overnight lights were flicking off, and people were up and moving. The livestock areas were bustling—horses and bears and whatever else they had there didn't like to wait until a decent hour for their breakfast, I supposed. But while their handlers might be the most awake, I didn't think that was the best place to start, since they'd also be the most distracted, and probably armed.

Sometimes, distraction was good, it got you information they didn't want to give, either verbally or through body language. But trying to wrangle a large-ish animal meant that any distraction could get someone hurt. I didn't want to risk that, when we had other options.

The midway, with its games of chance, was still shut down; it wouldn't come to life until mid-afternoon, when the gates opened to the public. And I wasn't quite ready to go barging into the living areas…not yet, anyway. Not unless we had cause to.

"Are you picking up anything else?"

"No. Just… we're in the right place. This is what I saw. But I don't, I can't *See* anything else."

"All right." I was getting soft, relying on her visions, anyway. Time to prove I deserved my license.

"Hey!" I raised my voice, and called out to a figure up ahead, carrying a long pole with what looked like a lash at the end. "C'mere a minute."

The boy turned and looked at us, and then with a shrug that clearly said whatthehell, walked toward us. He was in his late teens, sullen-faced and muscled in a way that suggested he didn't spend most of his day in front of the television—or a book, for that matter.

"You cops?"

Oh, the suspicious mind of a migrant worker. "If we were cops, we wouldn't have gotten this far."

The boy grunted, and gave Ellen a once-over. Her chin went up and she stared him back. His gaze dropped first. Whatever issues Shadow had, giving the other gender shit for sexism clearly wasn't on the list.

"We're supposed to find someone, figured you might know where they are."

"Maybe." Sullen didn't sound hopeful. "What's their name?"

"Don't know," I admitted cheerfully. "Don't know where they've been assigned, either. But they're mer." As I spoke I pulled my cap off and ran my hand through my hair.

It was a risk—this kid was human, not even Talent, and he might be a pure Null for all I could tell. But the fact that two fatae had been assigned gatekeepers meant the probability that this was an integrated crew was high.

"Mer?"

Bingo. The boy was playing dumb but his body language gave him away: he was ready to sprint in the opposite direction if I made one wrong move.

I spent most of my days passing—cross-breeds were rare enough that the fact that I'd lived as human my entire life trumped the obvious fatae aspects of my appearance. But I knew how to switch that out, at-need. I'd never look wholly faun, but there was no doubt that I was fatae.

Especially to a teenaged kid who—despite his sullen act—was no fool. His gaze flicked from my eyes to my horns, and then did a quick once-over, skimming along my body as though he were trying to adjust his initial perception. Then his gaze came back to my face, and I smiled. It wasn't, I admit, a pretty smile. In fact, I'd spent a lot of time practicing it to display just the right amount of arrogant shit.

"Mer," I said again. Two girls and a boy, teenagers."

There was a flicker, an awareness, and then something fell behind his eyes, and he took a step back. "I'm sorry. I don't know anyone like that here. Not too many of your folk around here, and none of 'em my age."

"Never said they were your age," I said softly. "Just teenaged.

85

Wide range, there." I could have been wrong, it could just have been the normal teen ego assuming everything revolved around them. But I didn't think so.

"Mister I swear, I don't know anything. There's nobody like that working here now."

"But there was, before?" I could feel Ellen tense beside me, but I didn't dare take my eyes off the kid to check on her. Some of the fatae, they could wring the truth out of you, like it or not. That wasn't my skillset. My glamour was hail-fellow-well-met, and it wasn't effective once they'd gotten skittish.

"Lots of kids come through. They think it's a glee, an easy gig for the summer. That they can drink all night and sleep all day and make money and then go home again when the summer's done. Most of 'em don't last a week. Mer wouldn't last a day, unless they were working the dunktank."

He wasn't wrong. But we also weren't looking for someone who was working here. Not willingly, anyway.

"Who does the hiring and firing?"

Passing the buck, Sullen could do. "Perkins. His office is back of the back, the one with the flags flying, that means he's in. I can go now? I gotta get to work."

"Yeah, go," I said, and he was halfway across the lot before I'd gotten the second word out of my mouth.

Ellen had seen me dead, too. And maybe dead here, or at least in danger, here, with a gun.

"How much control do you have?" It was way too goddamned late for me to be asking that.

She licked her lips, and rubbed the bridge of her nose, like it itched. "More than I did six months ago."

Not much of an answer.

"The first thing Genevieve did was teach me defensive spells. She said there were enough people eyeballing her and Sergei, I had

86

to be ready to duck and cover without her worrying about me, just in case."

That was a better answer. I reached around under my jacket, and pulled out my Glock. I hadn't needed to use it even for show in almost a year, and I didn't think I'd need it here... but the moment you weren't ready was the second you'd need it. And if she was seeing a gun, I'd rather it be mine than someone else's.

The grip was warm and familiar in my palm, my fingers curling around it as easy as clicking a mouse. I'd had the damn thing since I was in the academy, same as the boots on my feet. The boots had seen more use.

I checked the chamber, then reholstered the pistol. "Can you Translocate?"

She shook her head.

"Damn. Would have been useful. All right. Stay low and quiet."

I should send her back to the car, but that probably would be worse—I didn't trust the goons out back not to be stupid again, if they saw her alone.

The trailer was as advertised—four flags hanging limp over the roof: one American flag, one MIA, and two I didn't recognize. The door was open, a concrete brick holding it ajar. I knocked anyway.

"Yo, in."

The thing you learn, after a few years, is that most stereotypes and clichés become stereotypes and clichés for a reason. Perkins might've singlehandledly created the cliché of the stogie-smoking, scowl-faced carnie owner. I hadn't expected him to be Korean, but that was a minor dissonance in the cluttered, dingy office that also looked like the cliché of every carnie office, right down to the three generations out-of-date computer and the pile of fast food wrappers.

Perkins had a thing for Arby's.

"What can I do for ya?" He looked me up and down professionally, and I returned the favor. "Cop? Not local. Who're you looking for? I don't hire runaways, they're more trouble than they're worth."

I believed him. That didn't mean I trusted him.

"Not a cop. Private citizen." If he asked, I'd show him my I.D. but not unless he asked. He didn't. "Looking for three teenagers, traveling together. They came through here, we know that already so don't waste my time denying it. I want to know where they went."

There was a sound behind me, and Ellen stepped forward, not quite stepping in front of me, but fully visible. Out of the corner of my eye I saw her hands moving, a palms-up gesture that would have looked like a peace offering if you didn't know she was Talent. If you did, it looked an awful lot like she was gathering current. Perkin's gaze went to her hands, then to her face, and he let out a curse in a language I didn't know. Then, without warning, he broke.

"Bad crowd. Damned bad crowd. But the locals, they like their cut, and they're going to get it somehow, and a man's got to make ends meet, so I lease them space, every year." He scowled at me like it was all my fault, and a few things suddenly made sense.

"Cost of doing business," was all I said, though. Whatever deals he'd made with the locals, cops or criminals, human or otherwise, wasn't my business except if and as it led me to my targets.

"Yeah." His expression was sour, but his voice was as matter-of-fact as mine. Cost of doing business. When both cops and criminals require payoffs, what's a businessman to do?

"I threw them out, mid-season. Got to be too much, no matter how much money it brought in." He was sulky, not apologetic. I suspected they'd tried to undercut him, or something had gotten too expensive to pay off to cover up.

"So, my kids were with these people you didn't want hanging around your show. What were they doing?" The list of things a legit carny owner would spit at was pretty short, and matched with my expectation of where this case was going, but I wanted to put him on the burn, just a little

"I don't know. I didn't go into their tent. I didn't want to know." His body language flashed from annoyed to distinctly uncomfortable, and back to annoyed again.

"Don't ask, don't tell?" Ellen said, not really a question. "You knew something bad was happening, and you looked away."

There was something dark in her voice that hadn't been there before, not even when the current was flooding her system, speaking through her. My skin prickled, and I felt the urge to step away.

"El…" I said. Not a warning, not a question, just a reminder. We were in an enclosed space, a *metal* enclosed space, and she'd admitted that she didn't have all that much control yet.

"I saw them. I *Saw* them. And he looked away." She took a step forward, now ahead of me, standing between me and Perkins, and things had suddenly gone from in control to not in control.

"Where did they go?" I willed the idiot to answer me, and in detail. As much as I didn't want to cause a fuss here, I wasn't sure I'd be willing to get between a pissed-off Talent and her target, either, especially since she had a damned good point. If I thought it would do any good at all, I'd take him outside for a little come-to-Jesus myself.

"I don't know." His eyes shifted to the left, and I coughed. "I swear. But they've got winter quarters outside town. An old warehouse. I've never been there, ever wanted to go there, but it's all I got."

"Thanks ever so much for your help." The darkness was still in her voice, but it was tinged now with a note of snark that was pure

Sergei Didier. Wren might be Ellen's mentor, but her partner was leaving his mark, too.

That was both reassuring, and unnerving as hell.

9

Whatever I'd been expecting to find at the warehouse, this hadn't been on the list.

"A sideshow?"

"A freak show." I considered the neon sign, leaning against the car and crossing my arms against my chest, aware that—in my boots and baseball cap and leather jacket—I probably looked as disreputable as the building I was studying. Ellen was next to me, trying to mimic my pose and failing. It looked easy, but took years of practice.

"You think they have them there...." She looked puzzled. "Maybe... a front for prostitution? Or drug-running?"

"Maybe." I'd be surprised as hell if there wasn't some of both of that going on here. "But they've got an interesting cover. Freak shows are better suited to carnivals, not somewhere like this, where you don't get a lot of casual traffic. Even if they wanted to set themselves up for off-season customers, why not somewhere closer to a tourist area, where you get casual traffic? God knows, I doubt zoning laws would get in their way, if they're able to throw money around."

Ellen tilted her head, and made a face, understanding that this was a test. "Because there's something about this location that's important. Or they want to stay under the radar, here."

"And how do we find out?"

"We go in."

She didn't sound thrilled. I understood: when you're a freak yourself—and we both were, to the rest of the world—you were cautious about gawking at other freaks. Never mind that this was probably no different than any other Barnum-inspired funhouse with Fiji mermaids and mummified monkeys, and maybe a down on their luck fatae flashing a little wing or tail for the Nullbies.

"Seventeen bucks. There had better at least be an egress," I muttered. Ellen have me a confused look, but the woman taking our cash almost-smiled. I do appreciate a woman who knows the classics.

The first few rooms were the basics, the expected mummified monkeys, and what I was pretty sure was a piskie skeleton mislabeled as a tooth fairy. The thought of one of those kewpie-troll-doll menaces acting as tooth fairy was almost worth the $17 right there.

"Is that…" Ellen poked one finger at a glass case leaning over it to see better. "Is that a serpent's skin, like the one we talked to?"

"Yeah. They shed on a regular basis, when they're young. Might have washed up on the beach, or even been traded for something. Pretty, isn't it?"

"Prettier than when it's on it," Ellen said. She wasn't wrong: in the artificial light, the old skin glinted with a definite iridescent shimmer that the sea water had muted.

There was a scattering of other people walking through the rooms, one group of teenagers gathering around one case, giggling nervously, a father and daughter pair, dad making sure to keep her

92

smaller hand in his, no matter how she tugged to rush ahead, and an older couple, moving slowly, with evident pleasure, through the exhibits. And a woman, leaning against the far wall, near a sign that did, indeed, say "This way to the egress."

The employee saw me looking, and smiled. It was a carny smile. I sighed, and put on my best dumb mark expression.

"You like our exhibit?" she asked as I wandered over in her direction. Her nametag said she was Kerry, and she was good, mixing her professional shiller mode with an undercurrent of bored-with-this-job and a hint of actual physical interest. Just the thing to hook a male mark who needed his ego stroked by a little casual flirtation.

"It's okay." Casual, playing it cool, too cool to give in but definitely interested, even though I was there with someone. She wasn't human. She thought I was, though. "None of it's real, though, obviously."

"Yeah?"

"Please." I invested the word with male dismissive behavior, guaranteed to irk any female with a brain.

Ellen wandered up slowly, hanging back like she wasn't sure that she was welcome to join. I had a bad feeling that she wasn't playing—that she really was that unsure of her place, even now— but it worked too well for me to wave her closer yet. I'd apologize and explain later.

"You want to see something that'll really blow your world away?" Kerry said, her tone a come-on and a challenge, paired with one raised eyebrow.

I narrowed my eyes at her and cocked my head, playing the overly-confident rube. "And how much is it gonna cost me?"

She laughed, leaning in like she was going to tell me a secret. "High-rollers pay thousands, because they're suckers. For you?" She gave me another once-over, not even trying to be subtle. "For you, ten bucks more, that's all. Another ten dollars for the stuff tourists don't get to see."

It wasn't the best hook I'd ever heard, but I'd have bit no matter what. I pulled out my wallet, and counted out twenty dollars, handing it to her. She took the cash, and leaned back to press open a door that had been hidden in the wall behind her. "Go on in," she said. "Enjoy."

The door led into a landing, and then a short flight of stairs leading down. The stairwell was barren but well-lit, and the steps were clean and in good repair. I tensed up anyway, and reached back to take Ellen's hand, squeezing it once in warning before letting go. The door closed behind us, and I had the Glock in my hand, dipped down but ready. I didn't think this was a trap, but I didn't know *what* it was. Prepared was better.

At the bottom of the stairs there was no ambush, no guards, and no goons of any species waiting to get shot. There were, however, cases. Large cases and small ones, a dozen or so, each lit with professional quality lighting.

Gun still in-hand, I stepped forward and looked into the first case. A face looked back. My breath caught, even as part of my brain was categorizing what I saw, the way I used to scan a crime scene. Ridged forehead, pearlescent skin yellowed with age, eyes wide and milky-white, and a jaw that, dropped open, showed a double row of sharp, shark-like teeth.

A Nagini. Just the head, and a chunk of her neck: the muscled serpent's body missing, maybe lost, maybe cut off for easier display.

My throat tight, I moved on to the next case.

"Danny?" Ellen's voice was too small, too quiet, and I abandoned the display of what looked like a centaur's forearm to see what she had found. She was standing in front of one of the

94

full-sized cases, at the back, and her hands were palm-flat on the glass, as though trying to reach inside.

The case was set up like a diorama, with a painted backdrop of leaves, green and vibrant, while a three-dimensional tree trunk filled the center of the case, and in front of that...

No, not in front of. *Nailed* to the tree was the body of a woman, her skin smooth and brown, her arms twined above her head, her hair falling over one shoulder, down to her hips, her face...

God, her face.

Most people—Nulls, maybe even some Talent—would assume this was more of what was upstairs, frauds expertly done. I knew better.

"A dryad," Ellen choked out. "They did this to a dryad."

And another fatae had sent us down here, knowing what we'd see. Not that we had any great claim to the moral high ground compared to humans, overall, but... I'd trained myself to hold back emotion, to never let the anger interfere with the job. This took a hard shove, but it stayed down.

"Come on." I used my free hand to gather Ellen in closer, and we moved away from the ghoulish display, moving toward the back of the room, where a short hallway led us to another room, both of us bracing to find our missing trio, even as I prayed that I was wrong, that this wasn't what it was.

There were four exhibits in this room, each in a full, floor to ceiling case. And they were moving.

My first instinct was to break the cases, to free the beings inside, but Ellen's hand on my arm held me back. I looked back, and her face was strained, stressed, her eyes too wide and intently focused.

"Current," she said, looking at the half-dozen piskies fluttering around inside their case. "They're not alive, not really. Just...moving."

Magic. A Talent did this. Not that I had any particular love for the squirrel-sized tricksters of the fatae, but not even piskies deserved this.

And the other cases....

Ellen let out a harsh cry, and fell to her knees, a howl rising out of her throat that made me want to kill something, anything, just to feed the bloodthirst I could feel in that sound. The rage that escaped my control, finally, was cool and hard, implacable, and in need of something to hit.

In the other case, the largest one, were three mer, one perched on a rock, combing out her long green hair, the other two half-submerged, their tails flicking underwater, as though they were telling each other stories, or competing for her attention.

Ellen keened, and I dropped to my knees beside her, trying to keep my gun out and ready while still trying to offer some useless support, some reminder that she wasn't alone, my arm over her shoulders, holding her to me the way I would any injured, frightened child.

Too late. Far too late to save them; whatever Ellen had seen must have been echoes of their road to this place, this end. "Are they aware?" I didn't want to know, didn't want to ask, but I needed to.

"I don't..." She choked back a sob, the sound thick with phlegm and sorrow. "I don't know. There's..." She stared at the case as though trying to memorize it. "There's current there, but it's wrapped around them so tightly, I can't tell if anything's beneath any more."

Current was kin to electricity. Life ran on electricity, too, the pump of hearts, the tingle in our brains. The thought that they might be aware, turned into conscious waxwork displays to horrify and titillate... it was worse than any horror movie I'd ever seen, because it was real.

"Why?" So much pain in that voice, so much anger. "Why do I see things I can't change? What's the point?"

Everything she'd hoped to do, tagging along with me, had shattered. I wanted to comfort her, but there was no comfort in this room.

"We know what happened to them," I said. "There's no more uncertainty for their families. Sometimes, that's the best we can do."

It sounds weak, but being able to give a family closure can be enough. When you know it's not going to end well, having it end with even a small kindness…you take the gifts you get.

"Not enough. They change out the exhibits, the sign on the door out front said, new ones every six weeks." Ellen's voice was raw but clear. "This is new… they had others before. They'll have others again."

She looked up at the mer display, and something in her face changed, like the ocean had washed under her skin. "This is wrong."

On so many levels. But this misuse of magic, and fatae involved with the actual freak show, from the security to the door guard… it was going to get messy.

"We can sic the PUPs on them, but for now we need to keep moving." I could feel the time ticking down again—not for the teens, but for us. At some point, someone was going to start talking, and this place was not exactly the kind of place that liked official notice. If we wanted to bring them down, we had to make sure they didn't spook.

And I hadn't forgotten that she'd seen me dead, too.

"All right." Ellen got to her feet, wobbling a little, but her back straightened and her chin went up, and I didn't know how far it would carry her, but it was enough for now.

We made it as far as the exit—and this one had an actual exit sign on it, not egress—when someone came in through the out door.

"Not so fast," the person said. Perkins. And he had a gun, too.

"Oh, fuck me," I said.

Ellen had gone through too many emotional switches already. She'd been scared, and sad, and horrified and too many other things she wasn't quite able to grasp. When the carny owner confronted them, she reacted without thinking following not instinct—to hide—but the way Genevieve had been training her, to grab hold of her current and let it flow through her, opening herself up to it, so that she was ready to defend herself.

And when she did that, something pushed at her. Something large, not powerful in and of itself, but large enough to make itself known. It didn't feel like current, but it didn't *not* exactly, either. She tried to ignore it, keeping her gaze on the man in front of them, trying to see what Danny was doing, in case they had to make a sudden run for it, or if she was supposed to drop or-

That something pushed at her again, enough to slide through, a tendril, no, a gnat, biting at her, shoving something into her awareness, finding a tiny hole and forcing its way through.

"You bastard." She knew, suddenly, as though the mers had told her, their last whispers in her ear. "You sold them. You told them they'd have jobs, lured them here, and then you sold them!" Once she opened herself to it, the whisper grew into a wave, swamping her, explaining everything without having to say anything at all. The other fatae in the cases were too weak, their awareness too faint to start, or gone too long. But the mers were fresh, the magic animating them keeping electrical impulses running in their brain, too, enough that she had *Seen* them, *Seen* their despair, their sense of betrayal, the way they'd been moved from place to place...

They had called her here. Nobody else could hear them. Nobody else could do this.

Current hummed inside her, making her feel queasy, like she

was going to throw up, but at the same time like she could do anything, explode into violence like the ninja whatevers in the old movies her mother loved. Genevieve had warned her about that, about how dangerous is was to let current take control, that she could do more damage than she meant to.

She wanted to do a lot of damage. But Danny was next to her, and there were people upstairs, and she didn't know how to hurt only the right people.

"Just you?" Danny was saying, and she was confused at first, distracted by the current-hum, unable to focus well on the two armed men in front of her.

"Son, I don't want to be here," Perkins said, lifting his weapon until it was pointed directly at Danny's chest. "All you had to do was walk away, and nobody needed to be here, nobody needed to get hurt," he continued, like they were having a friendly little chat. "I told you the truth—I didn't want this anywhere near my show."

"But not out of any moral bias," Danny said, and his voice was dry, dry as paper, dry as winter air. "Just because things were getting too hot. Maybe the local inspectors got complaints? Comments that couldn't be ignored? There's always a small percentage of suckers who get too disturbed, who start to think, instead of reacting, and maybe some of them knew about the fatae, knew that your 'side show' was too real to not be real?"

"All it takes is one weak willy," Perkins said, "and the bribes cost more than what you're taking in. But I didn't like it, not once I knew about," and the tip of the gun moved slightly, taking in the entire basement, "this. Doesn't matter, didn't matter. Once you're in the game, you don't get to walk out again."

Ellen could see it all now, not the moment of death but just before, in that basement in the house by the Shore, the moment of realization when the girl cried out, desperate for something, for someone to know what had happened to her, to them, and the current had carried that call, dropping it into her brain, her core. It had all come from that, everything that brought them here.

There was no meaning to it, there was no hidden purpose. It was all chance, all random, who she heard, who she saw, flickers in the current-line, roads taken or not-taken.

Danny had moved in front of her, a subtle but clear protection, for all the good it would do, and was still talking. "So you're here to kill us, is that it?"

"Of course not," the man said. "Killing a human? That's illegal. Oh, wait. You're not human, are you?"

Fatae had no protection, because they didn't exist, legally. He thought she was fatae, too. But he had felt her pull current...

Ellen realized, suddenly, that Perskins didn't know about Talent. He knew about fatae, but not magic. He thought they were all the same, and his business partners had never told him anything else.

They were going to die. Die, and Danny would end up in one of these displays, and -

genevieve She didn't know if she could ping loud enough, over this far away, but she didn't know what else to do. *bonnie!*

The current sizzled and snapped around her, demanding that she do something. Something *now*, not waiting for someone else, hoping someone else will fix everything.

Random chance. But random chance that ended with her, *here*.

"Don't be a fool," Danny said, his voice tight and angry, but not scared, he wasn't scared, and he stepped forward and the gun went off, too loud in the basement room. Ellen dropped instinctively even before Danny's body hit hers, taking her to the ground, and then there was another gunshot, or maybe the echo of the first, and terror ripped through her, loosing the current in her core without any control whatsoever.

The glass cases shattered, and all she heard was screaming. Some of it might have been her own.

I hate getting shot. Never happened while I was on the force, but since then? Three times: twice in the leg, once in the shoulder. This made a third time in the leg, and it never hurt any less. The fact that I was pretty sure he'd been aiming for my chest wasn't much consolation.

The noise seemed to have died down, so I lifted my head and risked looking around. Underneath me, Ellen made a noise, and tried to get up, too.

"No. Stay down." I put my hand on her head, and kept her from looking. She didn't need to see this.

I couldn't use magic, but I could feel it. I was pretty sure head-blind Nulls a mile away would have felt this.

The glass cases were all shattered, the lights overhead likewise. The room was lit by a handful of emergency lights, the red glow adding to the surreal hellishness.

Perkins lay in front of us, face up. Or what was left of his face, anyway. Something had gouged at him, torn him apart, and left him in a puddle of... watered down blood.

I was pretty sure, without bothering to test it, that it was seawater. Poor bastard. He'd gotten too deep in bad things, but as much as I despised him, he wasn't the one who'd done this.

He'd been the one they could reach, though. Maybe. They? Maybe my Shadow had done this on her own. I didn't think so, though.

I'd leave figuring it out to the PUPs. My responsibility was to the living.

"Come on," I said, sliding my hand down to Ellen's shoulder. "Close your eyes, and come on. Trust me, and don't look."

She got to her feet, still shaking, and slid her hand into my

101

other one, twisting her fingers with mine. I tried to project as much reassurance as I could into my voice and touch, and slowly her skin warmed, her shaking eased.

"Your leg…"

"Hurts like hell, needs to be looked at, yeah. But not here. Let's go."

I'm not sure who was supporting whom, but we walked out of the exit and up into the lobby of the building. A few people stared, but nobody stopped us, as we walked out into the sunlight, and the car.

10

Most of my cases, I get to see the wrap-up. I'm the one who delivers a missing kid home, or tells the client good news about whatever they'd feared… or brings them the news they're never prepared to hear. Sometimes it's the best moment in the world, sometimes it's the worst, but there's always a sense of closure, that the agreement I'd entered into had been fulfilled.

I didn't have that, here. We'd gotten back to the city without incident, dropping the car off at the rental place and cabbing it, not back to my office, or the emergency room, but directly to the PUPI offices uptown. Bonnie'd been waiting, as had Valere and her partner, hovering with a mix of fear and anger. Valere had been almost maternal, swooping down on Ellen and wanting to know what had happened, if she was okay. The girl put up with it for a few minutes, stoic as an oak, and then broke down, wrapping her arms around her knees and putting her head down in a clear do-not-ask warning sign.

I didn't blame her a damn bit. I was tempted to myself. But Bonnie and Venec were waiting, and I needed to give them my report, so they could go do whatever it was they could do, to make sure this mess didn't get swept under anyone's' rug.

That's what PUPI was there for, to make sure magical crimes didn't get excused, explained, or otherwise forgotten. And if that meant that I didn't get to be in on the final moments... I was all right with that, for once. There wasn't anyone to tell: I knew that the sideshow'd already moved on, and finding them would be damned near impossible. Word would go out, because the *Cosa Nostradamus would* know, once PUPI was done. People—our people—would be alert, now.

Only what happened before I could say anything was that their office manager/medic took one look at me, and had me flat on my back and pantsless in under three minutes, possibly a world record. Only after she'd pronounced me bullet free and luckier than I deserved, and stitched me up, was Venec was allowed to take over. He was the thorough bastard I'd expected, wringing the last detail out of me until I almost wished the bullet had done more damage.

By the time I was turned loose, Ellen had been swept away by her mentor. I stood in the office lobby, my leg aching like a bitch, and feeling weirdly bereft. She had only shown up, what, 36 hours ago? If that? How had I gotten used to having a shadow, so quickly?

I hoped that Valere was able to help her deal with what she'd seen what she'd done, and headed home to a date with my case notes for the job Ellen's arrival had interrupted, a stool to put my leg up on, and a bottle of gin.

I don't drink often, but when I do, it's with the intensity and fierceness of my faun kin. And twice in one week added up, even for me. Which meant that when someone slammed on the door of my apartment at WTF early the next morning, I wanted to tell them to fuck off and die. Instead, I made sure I was wearing shorts—I was—and staggered to the front door. I didn't get hungover as easily as humans did, but there was some definite dehydration-exhaustion happening in my cells.

"Open the door, Danny."

I opened the door. My shadow stood there, looking about as good as I felt. But she was fully dressed, and carrying a box of what smelled like pain au chocolat.

"Come in," I said, but she was already in, handing me the box and stalking into the apartment like she owned it. I closed the door behind her, and leaned against it, holding the pastry box. Definitely pain au chocolat. My mouth watered, even as my brain demanded coffee. And my body wanted painkillers.

"Genevieve says twenty-four hours with you did more good for my control than a month of training," she said without any kind of hello or how are you. Although the latter was probably pretty obvious. "She says you're Earth to my Air, whatever the hell that means."

"Current and grounding." I knew that much about Talent, anyway. Air was current, earth was…well, earth. I looked down at the pastries in my hand, and saw not Valere's hand in this, but Sergei's. I didn't think well in the morning, but even I knew something was up. "Why are you here?"

Ellen turned and stared at me from across the entry foyer of my apartment. She seemed to suddenly notice that I was considerably underdressed, let her gaze drop to my feet, flushed slightly, and then kept her gaze trained on my face.

"It's all random," she said. "What I see, what I hear, it's not God sending a message, or people picking me because I'm me. There's no point to it except whatever meaning I can give it."

If she'd figured that out, she was well ahead of most of the world.

"So, I see the dead. No." She collected herself, started again. "I see those who're going to die, violently. I can't stop that, for whatever reason. And Genevieve...she can't help me, not with that. It freaks her out a little. It freaks everyone out. Except you." She swallowed hard. "I don't know why you're not scared of me, but you're not."

Maybe because I didn't understand it, all the potential she carried inside her, the way other Talent could. Maybe I was an idiot. But she was right: I wasn't scared of her, or what she did, or what she could do.

I should have been. If I'd any sense...

No, that wasn't right. I had plenty of sense. Maybe even too much of it. And Valere—and Didier—knew that. Fuck.

"I'm no mentor," I said.

"I have a mentor." She stared at me, not arguing, just waiting for me to figure it out on my own.

This was a really bad idea, on so many levels. I worked alone, she had no training, no license. No idea what she was asking for.

"This job hurts," I said. "Rip-your-guts-out hurt, sometimes."

"I know. God, I *know*. I don't want this. I never wanted this any of this. But I can't just," and she waved a hand in the air, unable to articulate whatever it was she couldn't do. "I can't not."

We stared at each other, while I tried to find a comeback to that, and failed.

"Only one way to screw up this game, rookie." My partner's voice, my first day on the street. *"And that's thinking whatever you do don't matter. Because everything we do, matters."*

"Fuck."

I may have said that out loud, because Ellen almost cracked a smile. I remembered the pastry box in my hand, and handed it to her. "Kitchen's over there. Go put these on plates and pour me some coffee while I put some damn clothes on."

Looked like my shadow was going to stick around.

106

Promises to Keep

107

for Kerry Stubbs
and Janet Gilman

1

The Thursday morning train was crowded, the weather was miserable with just enough rain to be, well, miserable, and we were coming up on a full week of non-employment. While I normally would never ill-wish anyone, it would not have bothered me if someone'd had something or someone go missing. At this point, I'd even take a stalk-n-snap job, just to have something to do.

Our office was a full block from the subway entrance. The rain had paused, but the air was still so damp with humidity, it almost didn't make a difference. My boots—acquired from a supply store in Oklahoma a decade ago—kept my feet dry, but my shirt was sticking to my back, and the cuffs of my slacks were soaked. At least I didn't have allergies—it seemed as though every other person I passed was sneezing and red-eyed from pollen.

I got off the elevator on our floor, took off my baseball cap and shook the dampness out of my hair, and checked my watch. Exactly seven fifty-eight. Well, at least I wasn't going to be late.

"Hey boss," a cheerful voice greeted me as I walked through the door at exactly seven fifty-nine. "Coffee maker's broken."

111

I stared at my secretary-slash-assistant-slash-not-quite-apprentice, and sighed. Of course it was. And the look on her face told me *why*. "What have I told you about using current in the office?"

"I didn't." Ellen sat behind her desk, now the very picture of injured innocence, which considering I was the one out a coffee maker was just damned unfair. "Your new client did. But I ran down and got you some from the corner cart."

I hung my hat and jacket on the tree, and glared at her. She picked up an unmistakable blue-and-white food cart cup from her desk, and offered it to me. Good girl. Not her fault that current— magic, if you're old-school—wrecked havoc with most appliances.

"New client, huh?" The coffee smelled of heaven, and had cooled down enough for me to hold the cup easily. I took a sip, and then looked around as though she might have stashed the client somewhere, ready to leap out at me once I was caffeinated.

The office still looked the same as it had when I'd opened Sylvan Investigations seven years ago, after I'd taken my twenty-and-out from the NYPD. The front room was clean but no-frills, a few potted plants clumped in the corner, waist-high and thriving, despite the fact that there'd never been a single ray of natural sunlight in this room since they put the walls up. The floor was polished hardwood, the walls were painted a non-industrial shade of sage green, and the wooden desk I'd bought at a fire sale for twenty bucks still sat in the middle of all that.

The difference between when I'd first set up shop and today was the desk was now covered with manila folders, a dozen different colored pens, an antique but still workable electric typewriter plugged into the best surge protector my money could buy, and anywhere from three to seven cans of soda in various stages of empty, depending on the hour of the day and how bad a day it had been. And the girl behind the desk, abuser of both the typewriter and the soda.

112

We'd been working together for four months now, since Ellen's vision of three kidnapped mer-children first brought us together. And by "brought" I mean she came to me asking for help, and I was dumb enough to give it.

Ellen was Talent, one of the magic-using humans of the Cosa Nostradamus. What earlier days had called a witch, a warlock, a sorceress. Me? I'm...not. Magic-using, or human. Despite that, we'd worked that first job together, well enough that her mentor, Wren Valere, had decided working for me on a regular basis would be part of her training.

Valere hadn't asked me first, of course.

"Drink your coffee, boss. Your horns are showing."

I don't know who'd taught her that was the fatae equivalent of calling someone a ditzy blonde, but I had my suspicions. If my office evoked a vague echo of the seedy-but-competent detectives of the 1940's—and I'm not saying it did, intentionally or otherwise—then Ellen could have swung the faithful Girl Friday. She wasn't particularly dishy, although she was young, and her style was more jeans and a sweatshirt than tight skirt and heels, but she had the sass down damn near perfect.

When it was just us, anyway. Other people came into the picture, and the uncertain, beat-down-too-damn-much shadow I'd first met made an unwelcome reappearance. But we were working on that, too.

"So," I prompted Ellen, leaning my hip against her desk. "New client?"

"In your office." Ellen handed me one of the files from her desk, while I, obedient, took another sip of coffee. "Mrs. Christina Eloise McConnell. A Ms. O'Sullivan sent her."

I remembered O'Sullivan. Her secretary had been hanging out with some rather nasty people who took things that didn't belong to them. She had been professionally grateful for my help—

apparently enough to send her friends along, too. I'm fond of former clients like that.

"What's the deal?" I asked, even as I flipped open the folder and scanned the top sheet. Ellen had better-than-decent handwriting, but she typed everything out so I could scan it into the files later. Having an assistant who was Talent—and therefore as likely to short out the entire office as get a file saved—meant I did more work, not less.

Fortunately, she had other skills and abilities that made up for it, when they weren't getting us into more trouble, anyway. But this seemed like a standard-issue referral, not what I'd come to think of as a Shadow Special, where her foresight got us involved.

"Missing husband," Ellen said, and then let me read the rest.

"Missing a full twenty-four hours, from… he disappeared from the roof?" I looked up from the report, surprised.

"Uh-huh."

"Well, that's different. And I take it her distress translated into our coffee maker going spoffle?"

Even when she smiled, Ellen looked serious. "Actually, she was detailing what he was supposed to be doing up on the roof, instead of disappearing, and it went spoofle. I don't think she's too happy with him."

"I can't imagine why," I said dryly, walking past the desk and opening the door to my inner office.

Mrs. McConnell was proof that you couldn't put a stereotype on Talent. She was in her late fifties, well-preserved in the way suburban ladies of a certain income level get, dressed in a tasteful suit and carrying a bag that you could have hid a mid-sized Chevy in. She was from Westchester County, where the wealthy don't-quite-flee NYC, though, so it was more likely a Prius, or a Volvo.

She didn't turn in her chair to look at me as I came in, but

114

waited until I had shaken her hand and introduced myself. Her gaze could cut glass, but her body language said she was more than a little embarrassed.

"I believe I owe you a coffee maker," she said.

I waved it off, pulling my chair out and sitting down behind my desk. "It happens. I take it you're calmer now?"

Either way, I wasn't going to take my laptop out of the shielded drawer until she left the office.

"Yes. I am sorry," she said, and looked it. I guess it was bad manners for a nice suburban lady to bust up a guy's coffee maker without having even met him yet.

Apologies offered and accepted, I was all business. "So, what can I do for you?"

Sylvan Investigations was, on paper, your basic private investigation firm. That meant that I took pretty much all comers, so long as they didn't smell too badly of trouble, and tried to find whatever it was they were missing, or track down what they feared was wrong. Nobody ever showed up in my office because they were having a good day.

But every PI has a specialization, even if they didn't advertise it. Mine was magic. Not the using of it—I'm no Talent—but the problems that came from it, the use and abuse. And for a Talent to be sitting in my office first thing in the damned morning, that was trouble with a capital T and that spelled Talent.

"My husband has gone missing," she told me.

"Off the roof of your house, yes." I placed the file down on the surface of my desk which, unlike Ellen's, was clear of everything. My citations and clippings were framed and hung on the wall, where everyone could see them and be reassured, and my pens and notebooks were secured in the drawer underneath my laptop, to be taken out when I needed them. I'd been raised to Navy standards, and some habits died hard. "He's been missing more than twenty-four hours, according to this. And the cops aren't interested?"

"They came to the house and looked around this morning, but there was no evidence of foul play, so they took down all his information and basically washed their hands of the matter. They told me to wait for him to come home. Or contact a divorce lawyer. You were a member of the NYPD yourself, Mister Hendrickson. You know how it works. He's a grown man, there was no sign of foul play, no ransom request or particularly odd behavior. They'll look—but they won't look very hard."

Unfortunate, but not unexpected. I had no doubt my former brothers-in-blue were running all the usual searches, but her husband, at least on paper, wasn't wealthy enough to be worth ransom, he wasn't important enough to have serious enemies, and unless a background search turned up something else, he was just another person gone walkabout. Kids, yeah. Kids and women, someone tended to take it personally. Middle-aged upper middle class white men, not so much. Not enough money to buy top billing, not cute enough to grab heartstrings, not ethnic enough to make good copy.

Unless this was a Talent thing. If the Cosa Nostradamus was involved, the cops up in Westchester wouldn't be much use, anyway.

"Do you have any reason not to believe that he simply Translocated off the roof, and hasn't thought to contact you?"

Not every Talent could Translocate, use current to move themselves from one place to another. I didn't understand the whys and wherefores of it at all, but apparently you needed a strong sense of self, plus what amounted to an internal GPS to get you there in one piece.

"Al couldn't have Translocated himself from the bathtub to the toilet." Her words were fond, not frustrated or disparaging. "He isn't high res at all—neither of us are, really. I suppose that's

116

why…" and she made a vague, slightly helpless gesture I took to indicate her encounter with the coffee maker. She hadn't been expecting it to happen.

High-res was someone like Wren Valere, or Benjamin Venec, who led the Cosa's only crime scene investigation team. Or my Girl Friday, sitting calmly outside doing filing for minimum wage and pizza every Friday. You couldn't ever tell from the outside. But strong emotions could do damage, even at a low level.

"Had your husband been upset, or worried about anything? Money problems? Personal problems?" The next question involved sexual problems, so I wanted to get everything else squared away before I had to go there. If there was a cause that didn't require me to hear the backdoor confessions from a client, I'd prefer that. Not that I'm a prude—pretty much impossible, considering my genetics—but I have a good imagination. Too good. And Mrs. McConnell wasn't my type.

"No." But she didn't sound certain.

I'm a good investigator. I'm well-trained, detail-oriented, and trust both my brain and my gut. But I have an advantage that a lot of other guys—and women—don't have. People *want* to like me. They *want* me to like *them*. It's nothing I do, nothing I've learned; it's just there, encoded into my genetics. Not being an idiot, I use it—carefully, but I use it. It's not tricky. Lean forward, look them in the eye. Basic moves that make the subject feel that you're engaged, that you do care—and then loosen the torque a little, the hold I keep on myself most of the time, and let some of that natural, damnable faun charm leak out. Just enough—like I said, she wasn't my type.

"I can only help you if you tell me everything."

"He… we've been married almost thirty years," she said. "And I know he's cheated on me. Not often, and never anything serious. They're one-night stands. He loves me."

She wasn't making excuses or justifications: these were things she *knew.*

"But I think…" She swallowed hard, and her forehead drew in, careless of the wrinkles it might leave. "I think one of the times he screwed up. I think there was a child."

"You think, or you know?" Had the mother—or the child—come sniffing around, looking to cause trouble?

"I think that he thought there was a child," she clarified. "He hadn't ever said anything, but there was a look on his face, sometimes. And he tried to find someone, once. Recently."

My finely-honed and trained investigative instincts—and my basic bullshit detector—told me that we'd gotten to the meat of it. "Someone?"

She reached into her bag of holding, and pulled out a plain gray folder. "He hired another investigator to find someone. A woman. I found the files a few weeks ago, when we were doing a renovation of the study, but… it didn't seem worth bringing up, then. Now, though… I thought it might be connected?"

I took the folder, and flipped it open. He'd gone to one of my colleagues, another ex-cop who'd hung out his shingle. Keith Hartman. Hartman was a decent guy, good at his job. Not in my league, but decent enough. They'd been looking for a woman, who seemed determined to stay just out of reach. Hartman's report went back three years: she'd lived in a rental apartment for the first year, then disappeared for a while, and then came back on the radar briefly, this time showing up on hospital records. And then she disappeared again, a little over eight months ago, about when our missing person starting asking about her. And that's where the trail apparently ended.

"Hospital. Maternity ward. And you think it was his?"

Mrs. McConnell gave an elegant, if helpless, shrug. "I think that he thought it was possible. But all he did was what you have; he

118

didn't push them to look more, or..."

And then he disappeared off the roof of their home. Taken alone, that was odd. Together with a mysterious woman and an unknown baby both disappearing off the face of the earth, it was odd enough to make my horns itch.

"You realize that, once I start looking, I might find things that are uncomfortable?" The kid, yeah, but also the fact that he had probably gone off of his own free will, without caring what his wife thought or felt. Or at least, not caring enough to clue her in.

Mrs. McConnell was a classy dame. She met my gaze square, and nodded once. "I understand."

The door opened, soft on its hinges, and Ellen tilted her head slightly, waiting to hear if she was going to be asked to run an errand, fetch a file, or clean up ex-former-client off the floor. Instead, Mrs. McConnell shook hands all around—even Ellen's which surprised Ellen a little, but she liked it—and nodded when Danny told her they'd email a contract that afternoon. They meaning he: she wasn't allowed anywhere near his laptop.

Then their new client was gone, and the boss exhaled once. It wasn't an unhappy or exasperated sound, more like he'd been thinking too hard to remember to breathe. Then he turned and went back into his office, leaving the door open. That meant she was supposed to follow him.

"So," she said, standing in the doorway.

"So."

Danny was sitting at his desk, his feet up, leaning back in the wooden chair at an angle. Every time Ellen saw him do that, she was convinced that he was going to fall backward and crack his skull open. It hadn't happened yet, at least not when she'd been around to see. She took the seat the client had just vacated, and tried to match his casual position, without actually putting her feet up. She thought that might be a bit much.

"Missing husband," he said.

"Off a roof."

He waved a hand airily, dismissing that aspect. "Either he was snatched off the roof by something winged, in which case we're probably not going to find him except as jumbo-sized pellets, or he went on his own. If he went on his own we have a chance."

"There are things large enough to take a grown man off a roof?" Ellen wasn't sure if he was joking or not. There were still things about this world, about the Cosa Nostradamus, that she didn't know, didn't understand. That made it painfully easy for others to punk her.

Not that Danny would. She thought. No, she was sure.

"Rocs, although they're not native around here," he was saying. "There was a native bird that could have done it but I'm pretty sure any still around aren't nesting in the suburbs. Dragons, natch, but if a great worm or even a lesser one took him, we're done."

Dragons she knew about. Not quite first-hand but close enough. A distance of about two miles—this distance between Madame's townhouse an their office—was close enough.

"So where do we start?" They'd had a missing person case before, but that had been a pair of teenagers who'd run off together, what Danny had called good starter material. This sounded like it would be more complicated.

"With what our missing man was looking for. Or rather, what he was rather carefully not looking for."

She really hated it when the boss got cryptic. It meant he was making shit up as he went, again.

2

When Ellen had first started working with Danny Hendrickson, she'd been relegated to following and watching. His shadow, he called her. This time, though, she had gotten handed her assignment, and sent off to do it. Alone. That made her feel triumphant for about ten minutes.

Most of investigation work, Ellen had quickly learned, was incredibly boring. On the other hand, it could be worse; at least she got out of the office. Danny took all the on-line research, because he was less likely to short out their entire office with one misplaced burst of frustration. Bad enough they were going to have to buy a new coffee maker: if they had to buy a new printer and laptop, the budget would be fried, too.

Doing legwork wasn't exactly glamorous, though.

"So, what's this guy's name again?"

"Alfred McConnell," she said, trying not to lean away. Chadwick was a good guy, as things went. Human, Talent, and generally happy to help out, he was her first stop not because she thought he'd know anything pertinent, but because talking to him wasn't particularly stressful, and she needed all the confidence-building she could get.

She just wished he'd stop trying to look down the neck of her sweater.

"Huh. Nope. He's local work?"

"Westchester."

She might as well have said Mars; Chadwick shook his head and pushed the photo back to her. "Sorry, Ellen. You know me, I don't work much above 96th Street."

"Yeah, I figured, but you're the first stop on the list, as always."

He took that as a compliment to his knowledge, and preened a little. Ellen kept her expression professional-tough, but inside she felt a giggle shake free. The first time she and Danny had come to see Chadwick , she had been terrified; other Talent were still a mystery to her, and men—especially older men—way out of her league. But then Danny had introduced her as Wren Valere's mentee, and the other man had practically bugged his eyes out, and said "'ma'am," until she'd rolled her eyes and told him to call her Ellen.

She knew Genevieve was powerful, and well-respected—and with reason. She also knew that Ellen herself was, by the standards of the Cosa Nostradamus, and as Talents judged things, almost as powerful. But she didn't *feel* powerful. And Ellen's real power, the reason other people were cautious around her, and treated her with respect, wasn't anything she could control, or consciously use. Her StormSeer sense was external rather than internal, some intense need reaching out to her through the natural strands of current, a ley line, or thunderstorm.

This case had none of that; she had intentionally walked through Central Park, over a known ley line, to make sure. Not even an itch of foreboding, not a single vision.

Ellen knew that she should be thankful: her visions tended to

122

end badly. And yet… she felt somehow useless, like *not* seeing their client in imminent mortal danger meant she'd let Danny down somehow.

Sergei, Genevieve's partner, said she suffered from a Surfeit of Insecurity Syndrome. He had smiled when he said it, but he hadn't been joking, not really.

"The person you should talk to," Chadwick said, thoughtfully, almost unwillingly, "is Madame Haddad."

Haddad. Ellen sat back in her chair and considered the other Talent. She knew of her by reputation, but had never met the other woman. She was a power-broker, a matcher. Genevieve had never worked with her, because she had Sergei, but her mentor had said she was good at what she did, matching people, Talent, up with clients who needed their particular skills.

"You think–" she started to ask, when Chadwick spoke over her.

"I'm just saying that she's got a finger on the pulse of everything that goes down. If this was anything more than a guy taking a flying leap into nowhere, she'd have the skinny."

"Ellen Bint al-Genevieve"

Getting an appointment to see the woman had been as simple as showing up and asking the receptionist if Madame Haddad was in. She hadn't even given her name; she hadn't thought it necessary. She'd been right.

Mahiba Haddad was tall, elegant, and very old. Her suit was perfectly tailored, her headdress a delicate length of silk that covered her hair and draped loosely around her shoulders. Her eyes were the same dark brown as Ellen's own, but her skin was paler, olive-toned.

"Madame Haddad." There was an awkward pause, and then Ellen sat down in the chair opposite the desk, folded her hands on her knee, and waited. Ellen didn't know the phrase the other

123

woman had used, but in connection with her mentor's name, she assumed it was some variant of "daughter of." Genevieve was only about a decade older than Ellen, and not exactly mother material, but from what Ellen had learned, the mentor/mentee relationship trumped everything else, with Talent.

"Call me Mahiba, please," the older woman said now. "I had not thought to see you here, in my office. Certainly not for many years yet."

"I am not here for myself," Ellen said carefully, wary of accidentally making any agreements. "Merely as proxy for another." If there was going to be any cost to this, financial or otherwise, Danny could cover it. That's what the boss was for. "A man named Alfred McConnell has gone missing."

"And you are searching for him. What makes you think that I might know of this man?"

Both Danny and Sergei said: listen more for what someone doesn't say that what someone does. Mahiba hadn't said no, or she didn't know, or that she couldn't help. "Mr. McConnell went missing while searching for another. But he was not the sort to dig into dark corners on his own."

Ellen heard herself falling into a more formal voice, echoing the other woman's speech patterns. Sergei had taught her that, and Danny encouraged it. Echoing showed respect, attention.

That was the theory, anyway. Ellen was always afraid that it would come across as mockery.

Mahiba did not seem to feel mocked. She nodded gravely, and reached across her desk to pull a great leather binder toward her. Ellen immediately felt a surge of envy: Danny had his computer, but she had been working in cheap spiral notebooks and lined pads.

"McConnell. Talent, yes. Male, white, searching for someone who had been lost to him. I gave him three names. Hartman, Louis and Hendrickson."

Ellen started and Mahiba smiled grimly. "No, he did not choose your partner."

"It would have simplified things considerably if he had. He also might've found who he was looking for."

"Why do you assume he did not?"

She smiled at Ellen's expression, then picked up a pen and wrote a series of lines, gently pulling the sheet out of the book and passing it to her.

Ellen took it carefully. The ink glinted wetly on the page, drying as she read it. And then read it again, and said, under her breath, "Oh *hell*."

This was important enough to take straight to Danny, and not wait on their scheduled check-in. The problem was, going back to the office would be half an hour at least on the subway, and he might not even be there when she arrived. So she stood on the street, new information in her pocket, and frustration building in her. Stupid, *stupid* not to have planned for this.

She chewed on a nail, and tried to think of a solution.

Once upon a time, she'd been told, there were working public phones on the streets in New York City. Now, the booths were mostly dismantled shells, and everyone had cell phones. Everyone except Talent, anyway, because current—specifically, the current held within her core—would short out every bit of a cell phone carried anywhere near a Talent, over time. And "time" could be anything from a year to five minutes, depending on the Talent. "Stay calm, Ellen." That had been Genevieve's first lesson. Stay calm, and make sure you're in control of your core, where the magic rested. A Talent who couldn't control her core was a danger to everyone. Bad enough if she shorted out a city block, or set something on fire—but now, to do so would shame Genevieve, too. The idea that people thought she was worth training, worth

125

hiring, was still so new that she'd rather lose an arm than embarrass any of them, most especially her mentor.

As soon as she thought that, she had her solution. *genevieve?"*

It wasn't a word, exactly, or even a thought. It was more, if she had to describe it, like the *sense* of her mentor, the visual remembrance and the sound of her voice and the taste of her current crackling in the air, shaped into a dart that she launched into the faint eddies of current that swirled around them, all the time. It was called "pinging," and it was the closest thing Talent had to instant messages.

Some people were better at it than others. Some could send a ping that seemed as though it were typed on a page, clear and crisp. Most people, though, it was more muted, more generalized, an emotional push of "are you okay?" or "meet me here." Ellen didn't have enough control or experience yet to manage anything more than a vague sense of her message, and only to people she knew well enough to "find."

what's up? came back immediately. Genevieve was alert, but not worried, a sense of ready-to-act rather than in-motion-already.

danny Ellen sent back, focusing on the need to talk to him, rather than there being a problem. Most of what they did was confidential. She couldn't share what she'd learned, *can't call.*

A sense of comprehension hit her in return, and the knowledge that Genevieve was passing the buck to Sergei. Her partner was a Null, and could—and did—carry a cell phone.

Ellen sent back a ping of relief, and gratitude, then *going to grab coffee at the dog," a coffee shop in the area. She'd wait until she heard back from Genevieve, or Danny found her.

3

When I took Ellen on as my assistant-slash-student, I'd also added Sergei Didier's phone numbers- both his private one and the gallery's main line—into my cell phone. It wasn't any kind of premonition, just common sense. Having it appear on the display for the first time today, after sending Shadow off on her own, had nearly given me a heart attack, though. Considering his first words were "nobody's dead," he'd known what my reaction would be.

"We need a better set-up." I said as I slid into the booth opposite Ellen.

Ellen looked up from the laminated menu she'd been studying, and gave me a Look. "What, carrier pigeons?"

The girl who'd first approached me, months ago, nearly shaking from the weight of the vision she'd seen, ready to shrink away from anyone or anything that looked at her harshly, wouldn't have snarked like that. Or rather, she would have, but it would have been a defensive move, a deflection, a way of showing armor and warning away would-be predators.

Now, she was just snarking because she could. Despite my

exhaustion, I smiled. Long way to go, still. But progress.

"It couldn't be any less awkward than having to relay everything through those two," I said, but I didn't have any brilliant plan to offer, either. "You could have borrowed someone's landline, you know. Go into a store and ask if they've got one. But buy something, first."

Even as I made the suggestion I knew it wasn't going to fly. Ellen could snark at me, but she *knew* me. Walking into a strange place, and asking for what was, in effect, a favor? She'd grown up in a house where she was considered odd, if not outright crazy, and everything she said or saw was doubted and ridiculed. Talking to strangers—people who might judge her—was still a trigger, even now that she knew that magic was real, the fatae were real, and she wasn't crazy at all. Or at least, no more so than the rest of us.

I wasn't her therapist or her mentor, anyway. Just her boss. "So what have you learned?"

"I have a lead. On the person our missing person was looking for, anyway."

I waited. There had to be more to it than that, some kicker that had made her haul me out here, rather than waiting. She shook her head, and pushed a sheet of paper across the table toward me. I took it, unfolded it, read it.

You learn to roll with the punches, the jobs I've had. Never show what you're thinking, much less what you're feeling. Even when they know they've gut-punched you. Maybe especially then.

"So," I said, when I could finally trust my voice again. I lifted my hand, summoning the waitress over. "Coffee, black, and a plate of rye toast," I ordered. It might be iced coffee season for everyone else, but I'm an old-fashioned boy.

"So," Ellen echoed, waiting on me.

"Our missing woman was fatae," I said.

"Yep."

128

"So our missing man has a cross-breed daughter."

"Looks like."

Cross-breeds are rare. Trust me on this, I know.

My coffee came, and I wrapped my hands around the mug. The toast my stomach had been grumbling for minutes earlier didn't seem quite so appealing, but I knew better than to put more coffee on an empty stomach, so I lifted a piece, and took a bite. I should have stopped for lunch three hours ago, especially since I hadn't been getting much in the way of results.

"It's all there, everything Mahiba knew," Ellen went on, her voice soft, like she thought I was going to tell her to shut up at any moment. "She gave birth at St. Luke's, before they shut it down. She checked out without the baby."

Not unusual. St Luke's used to handle a lot of the fatae in town. The unusual thing was that the fatae had gone through with it at all. No, what was unusual was that she had caught, and then that she had gone through with it. Maybe she hadn't realized the baby had a human father? Who knew. Sometimes, fatae could be such careless sluts.

I didn't realize I'd said that out loud until I heard Ellen's indrawn breath of reaction.

"We are," I said, ruefully, and took another bite of the toast. It was pretty good, with just enough butter to soften the crunch. "God knows, my father…. Well, fauns are fauns. Probably not the best example. Do we know what breed she was?"

"Not in the notes."

"She was human-shaped, at least, or even St. Luke's might have noted something was up when she walked, and called in the Cosa, which would have put this on my radar." Like I said, cross-breeds were rare. Someone would have made sure the only other cross-breed in the city would have known, right? Although what they'd have expected me to do with that knowledge, I don't know.

"Right. So, what do we know? Only that our client's missing husband disappeared off the roof, after, how long ago?"

"Eight months," Ellen supplied.

"Eight months after he went looking for what we now know to be a cross-breed infant, presumably his, because why the hell else would he care?" My issues were showing.

"Presumably his." Ellen still had that scrunchy look going between her eyes. "Is this going to be a problem, boss?"

"No." It wasn't. "If anything, I mean, the guy's actually looking…yeah, he's late, but at least he's making an effort now." The older I got, the more I understood that sometimes you just…couldn't do anything right away. It never got easier to *accept*, but you understood.

She played with the spoon in her hands, thinking. I let her be. Part of learning is figuring stuff out by yourself. When she had a question, she would ask. I finished my toast, and then ate what was left of her share. I was the boss, I was picking up the tab, I could eat all the toast if I wanted to.

"Do you think he knew? I mean, that she wasn't human?"

"Yeah. You can pass"—I did all the time, just pull on a baseball cap and turn my head so my features seemed softer, more human, that sort of thing "- but once you're that up close and personal, it's pretty much impossible to hide."

"Do you think it's connected? I mean, the woman, the baby, and him going AWOL off a roof? There's almost a year between the two things."

I wiped my fingers, and crumpled the napkin and dropped it on my plate. "Second law of disappearances: if something unusual happened in the missing person's life in the year previous, odds are high it's connected."

She nodded, taking that in. "And a cross-breed offspring is unusual."

130

My usual response would have been sarcasm, but I couldn't bring myself to it. "Considerably higher on the weird-o-meter than disappearing off a roof without any sign of climbing down." The first law of disappearances was that the nearest and dearest almost always had the motive with the mostest. Although that was the first rule of pretty much everything.

"Boss, what are we getting into? I mean, is this a two-person-missing case, or…"

Or what, was the question. Or what seemed to always be the question. I should have listened to my mother and gone into the Navy. At least there you knew the shape, color, and requisition form for whatever shit you were handed.

"Damned if I know, kid." This was why I never promised the clients anything except my best effort; because every job inevitably went pear-shaped, in its own way. Focus on what we know, and what we were hired to do. Find our guy. He was chasing the baby, so where did the baby go?" I watched as she hauled out her spiral-bound notebook and flipped to a fresh page, ready to take notes—or, as I'd learned was more probable with Ellen, to sketch a flow chart. She thought in weird ways, even for Talent.

"If the mother walked out without the baby, she didn't want it," she said. "So it's unlikely that she went back for it later. We can probably rule her out, either as a problem or an answer."

She started with a box connected to a triangle by a dotted line, then a line from each to a circle. Mother and Father and Baby make Three. Then a line away from Baby Circle, with a question mark. "The baby wasn't adopted—would it have been an obvious fatae? Is there a fatae adoption board, or something?"

"No. A fatae baby's always taken in by its family—extended or otherwise. Or, it…"

There was a very uncomfortable silence.

"Or it's left out to die?" she asked softly.

I'd promised not to coddle her. "Mostly, yeah. Although not often, I'd think. Population shrinkage means most babies are wanted, even with human blood."

Most, not all. And a cross-breed? If the fatae parent didn't want it, the human parent had some hard decisions to make. For one: how did you deal with it if Junior or Princess didn't look human enough to pass?

Ellen was either reading my mind, or thinking along painfully similar lines. "Your mom…"

"My mother was pretty amazing," I admitted, not looking at her. From what little I'd been told, and the little I'd figure out on my own, Ellen's folks hadn't been amazing. Not for her, anyway. This case was going to open up some holes underfoot, no matter what we did.

"And…your dad?"

"Never met him." The burn that should have caused had died out a long time ago; I didn't even twitch any more. "My mom was in town for Fleet Week. He was a good-looking bartender. She shipped out without knowing she was pregnant, and…" And then came me, and the rest of her career behind a desk.

"Did she know he was…"

That made me laugh, and it felt surprisingly good. "There's no way you can't know. Horns, hooves, tail… and, apparently, endless stamina." She hadn't told me that part, I'd learned that one on my own. "Yeah, she knew. I think she thought you couldn't cross-breed."

Ellen shook her head, looked compassionate and disapproving the way only a woman can. "There should be PSAs."

"Absolutely. There should."

And that was about as far as we were going to go into interpersonal traumas as they related to this case. I finished my coffee, and pulled out my own notebook. Across the table, Ellen was still sketching out her own thoughts. Her notebook was a lot

132

neater than mine, with colored tags and clearly lettered lists from previous jobs. My handwriting was still a disgrace. Of course, I got to enter most of it into the computer at the end of the day: she still had to read hers a week later.

"The missing guy's last few weeks visible were normal? Nothing unusual, nothing downright weird?" I knew already, but I was learning that bouncing questions off Ellen sometimes got me, not new answers but new questions.

"By various parameters of weird, no. He was retired, did a lot of puttering around, the way retired people do. Spent a lot of time at the hardware store, which I guess is normal for a guy planning on cleaning out his own gutters and doing some repair work? I don't think—"

She stopped talking, her normally sleepy-lidded eyes going wide, looking at something miles past my shoulder. Her lips opened slightly, as though she were going to say something and then forgot, and her dark skin went ashy underneath.

I'd never wanted to be a Talent. In fact, I'd occasionally given thanks that I *wasn't*. But maybe, if I were, if I could feel the current moving the way they did, I'd feel less helpless when Shadow had a vision.

I picked up my jacket, ready to shove it under her if she started to slump, and waved off the waitress who was coming over with more coffee, but otherwise, all I could do was wait.

Ellen had come to me in the first place not because she wanted to be a PI, but because she saw dead people. People who were going to die, really, but by the time someone found them…. She wanted to improve the odds. Get to them before they died. And I needed to keep people from coming to bad ends. It had seemed like a good match.

The problem was, the visions came when they did, and weren't much concerned with anything else Ellen might be doing.

As quick as it hit, it seemed to leave. Color came back to her skin first, like her heart had paused pumping blood and was only now picking up again. It took another minute before that glassy thousand-yard stare started to fade. Then she blinked, exhaled, and came back to now.

I had already flipped to a new page in my notebook. She'd only had one vision since the first one that brought us together, at least that she'd told me about, but you followed the same rule of interviewing any eyewitness—you wanted to get them talking before they had time to think about what they had seen, putting their own spin on the facts.

She focused on me, and started talking. "Two men. One black, one…white? Maybe. Similar, but different. Younger than you, but not by much. They're scared. So scared, and something's coming for them, something casting a shadow, a huge shadow from above."

I wrote down everything she said, exactly, even as my own brain was putting a spin on it. Two men, different races, somewhere in their early thirties. Probably. I aged more like a faun than a human, so to outside eyes I passed for late thirties, even with the silver showing up in my hair. Human—Ellen knew to identify if they were fatae or not, unless they were so human-shaped they had no distinguishing characteristics, and there weren't many of those—as we'd just been talking about, even I couldn't pass, if you were looking close. And a large shadow, from overhead…

That could be anything, I warned myself, focusing again on what she was saying.

"They're not dead yet. Their skin is warm, they're breathing."

One of the things we'd been working on was teaching her to separate herself from the vision, to pick out details without losing the overall sense. But all the dry runs and tray-tests in the world won't tell you how it will work in practice. So far, so good.

"And there's this sound… dry. Dry and fast. Like…" She

squinted her eyes shut, trying to recapture it, and I flipped the notebook closed. Nothing she said after this would have the clarity of her first words.

"Like cicadas," she said. "Like a thousand cicadas."

It was the wrong season for cicadas to flock. But I knew what else made that noise.

"All right. Let's go check that out."

Ellen gave me another Look. "We're on a case."

"And you had a vision. The missing take second place to those in imminent risk of death."

The missing might also be in danger of imminent death. She didn't point that out. We had an understanding. Or rather, I had an understanding, and she understood that she didn't have a say in the matter.

"You need to go after—"

"It's one thing to run down separate leads. Another entirely to split up cases. You're not ready yet to do this on your own."

I'd nicknamed her Shadow for a number of reasons, part of which was because that's what she was supposed to be doing. Shadowing me, learning. Not haring off with her heart askew and her brain still vision-fogged.

"Alfred McConnell can wait," I told her, and hoped to hell that was true.

4

Cart Hollow was one of those suburban New Jersey towns that you only knew about if you lived there, or knew someone who lived there. Bedroom communities, nothing more than houses and schools, no reason to go there if you didn't already live there. Most of the residents worked in the city, commuting on a daily basis and bringing their considerable paychecks home to spend. People were nice, polite, but they weren't accustomed to strangers walking up to their door and ringing the bell, especially mid-morning on a weekday.

The man waiting at the door had thick black hair that was running heavily to silver, the face underneath handsome enough but starting to show signs of wear. If he'd been wearing a suit and tie, he could have passed for a lawyer, or maybe a banker, the kind that dealt with individual clients, managing money rather than making deposits. But he had on paint-splattered jeans, sneakers, and a red Rutgers sweatshirt, instead.

"Please," he said. "Let me see her."

"Her who?" The owner of the house shook her head, holding her

136

body between the doorframe and the door, just in case he tried to rush her, to get inside. "Man, I don't know what you're talking about."

"Please. All I want to do is see her. To make sure that she's all right."

The door closed in his face, not roughly but firmly, and he stepped back off the stoop. The house was a nice one, a narrow, four-story rowhouse, still zoned for single use. The steps and front yard were small but well-maintained, the paint was fresh, and the man who had answered the door looked like a college professor type, no obvious tats or scars, or any indication that he was holding anyone against their will.

Not that a baby could have much will, and facades were deceptive. He knew that for a fact.

"I just want to see her," he said to the house. "I wouldn't take her away from you, not if you love her." He was too old to raise a child now, even if Christine were willing—and she probably would, he'd lucked out and married a woman with enough heart to deal with him. He just wanted to see her, to know...

He turned to his companion. "Are you sure that she's here?"

It nodded. It was sure. That was why it had brought him here.

"All right. Then we'll keep trying."

He owed it to the child's mother, if nothing else. He'd failed her before, hadn't known about the child, hadn't been there when the child was born. He had to make sure the child was safe.

Stepping back onto the sidewalk, so the residents couldn't complain that he was on their property, Alfred started to walk away, his companion at his side. The fatae hadn't left him alone more than thirty seconds, including bathroom breaks, since swooping him off the roof, as though it were afraid the human would run.

Where would he go, if he ran? Even assuming a sixty-something human could outrun a winged fatae—unlikely—where would he run to? Back home, where the creature had found him in the first place? This creature was, for whatever reason, also interested in his daughter—and the word was still so impossible, so unexpected, it made his heart clench when he thought it.

No. He had gotten nowhere eight months ago, hiring a detective, had gotten nowhere playing the usual bureaucratic phone tag. If this fatae who had not given him a name, had not told him anything other than it too had an interest in finding this child, that it could help…

Then he would do whatever it asked. Even if it did seem, so far, to involve harassing the alleged adoptive parents until they could prove that the girl wasn't there.

"Sir?"

He looked up, and up. Two of New Jersey's Finest were in front of him. They didn't look happy.

His companion was gone, of course. Alfred hadn't heard it leave, any more than he'd had warning when it swooped down on him, feathers glinting in the sun.

"Is there a problem?" The moment he said the words, he knew they were the wrong ones. "Can I help you?" would have been better, innocent citizen with nothing to fear. Asking about a problem implied that there was one.

"You don't live around here?"

"I…no." He lived well north of here, in another state entirely. And he didn't have a car to get into, to leave, couldn't point to the mass transit he'd used to get out here, had no excuse for being here that wouldn't land him in trouble. Sixty-plus years of being a law-abiding citizen, and he had no way out of this one.

"Do you have some identification on you, sir?"

"I…" he made a motion for his back pocket, but knew it was useless. He'd been working on the roof, who brought their wallet with them when they were doing home repair chores? In his old workboots, weekender jeans, and sweatshirt, he could have been anyone, from a comfortably-retired banker doing chores to a homeless person.

One of the cops looked up and down the street, obviously looking for something. The other one took a step back, indicating their patrol car. "If you'll come with us, sir?"

He went with them.

They were very polite, asking him again what he was doing there. He shook his head, and couldn't tell them. How did he get there? He shook his head again. He waived his phone call—what would he do, call Christine and tell her…what? No. Better to wait. He would say nothing about feathered companions, or stolen changeling babies. He hadn't done anything wrong. Eventually, they would decide he was harmless, if a little crazy, and let him go.

Eventually—after they gave him a half-stale turkey sandwich and a decent cup of coffee—that was what happened.

"You want a ride to the station?" Officer Breidbart asked him.

"No, I'm good," Alfred said. "I think I'll walk."

He knew Breidbart was watching him. They had pointed out where the train station was, only a few blocks away. They had given him a schedule, and a twenty dollar bill to get him home—or somewhere that wasn't their town. He couldn't fault them in any regard.

He also knew that there was no point in going back to the house, even if he could find it. If the child had been there, she was gone now. It had been the pattern at the last three houses they had gone too, as well. His companion—captor? guide?—could scent the child somehow, although it had a beak rather than a nose, but it could not gain entrance to the house. It needed Alfred for that.

So he kept walking, and waited for his companion to find him again.

Ellen tried to stare her boss down. It was doomed to failure—she couldn't meet anyone's eyes long enough to win a contest like that—but she gave it the best shot she could.

"You're getting better."

"Fuck you."

That she could say that, mutter it really, still surprised her. She wouldn't dare say that to Genevieve, or Sergei, or anyone else. Well, she might say it to PB, the demon who was her mentor's best friend, but PB took that sort of thing as his due.

Danny pulled out his cell phone and told it to call someone nicknamed Bookpusher. Ellen didn't exactly slide across the bench to get away from the phone, but she might have shifted a little backward. Instinct: the more current she used, the more a menace she was to electronics, and cell phones were among the most sensitive.

"'Pusher, hi. How much do I owe you, right now? Yeah? Okay, add to the pile." He pulled the sheet of paper toward him and fact-checked himself, then said "St. Luke's, between six and twelve months ago. All female infants born there, no matter what happened to them after. Yeah, preemies, stillborns, Apgar 10s and everything in-between. Can you do that for me?" He paused. "Woman, if I had a name, I could do this myself."

Bookpusher had something to say to that, apparently. Danny leaned his head against the back of the booth, the phone held to his ear, and tried to look like he was paying attention.

"All right, okay. Yes, you're brilliant, you're wonderful, and we're now up at the fly-you-to-Rome for that dinner stage of IOUs, I get it. Just compile the names and who they went home with, if they went home. Yeah, if they didn't go anywhere I need to know that, too."

Ellen thought that maybe Alfred McConnell would have known if his daughter died at birth. But then again, he hadn't hired Danny, or gone to Mahiba to ask. So maybe he didn't even know where she'd been born, to check. It must be awfully easy to lose track of a baby, if you didn't even know where it had been born.

"You're, as always, the light in my research darkness. Talk to you soon."

He hung up the phone, turned it off, and put it back in his pocket, muffling the jangling chiming noise it made as it shut down. His hand came out again with something else in his fingers.

"Tell you what. We'll flip a coin. Heads, we keep on with the case. Tails, we hunt down your vision. Deal?"

That was insane. But Ellen just shrugged, having used up her store of protest already.

He flipped it elegantly into the air, catching it flat on the back of his wrist. Heads. Danny tilted his wrist, and the harsh overhead light caught the metal, making it glitter.

"So, right. Vision it is."

5

The subway took us into Brooklyn, letting us off a few blocks from our destination, and we walked the rest of the way to the cemetery in silence. I avoided the main entrance, skirting to the side. The arch overhead was massive, easily three times as high as a tall adult, and wide enough across for two cars to pass, one going in the other heading out, without risk of scratching. It was marble, what looked like one single piece, and deeply carved with images that had been worn down over the past two hundred years to where they were only lovely shadows.

"The main entrance is worse," I told her. "I mean, glorious, but worse. And too many people. It's better to slip in quietly."

"This is the back door?" Ellen looked up at the archway as we walked under it, and shook her head. "Once you're dead, you don't much care, so why–"

"It's not for the dead. Cemeteries are for the living." There was no other reason the grass on either side of us was trimmed as lovingly as a golf course, or the huge trees ringing each section were so gorgeously placed, creating a dappled oasis of shadows and cool even on the warmest summer days.

"It feels like it should be a college campus, or park, or something."

"It used to be. Well, sort of like a park. Back when, people came here every weekend for picnics."

"Ugh."

"Yeah well, not to my preference either, but green spaces are green spaces, and hey, why not come to visit grandma while you were at it?"

We'd been walking along one of the side paths as we talked, skirting around a funeral in progress down at the bottom of the hill. I had a destination in mind, but was taking the indirect route. It was polite, when dealing with certain sects of the Cosa Nostradamus, to make like you'd stumbled on them by accident, rather than taking the straightaway.

We heard them first. Or, I heard them, and from the way my Shadow stumbled on perfectly smooth grass, I was guessing she did, too.

"That's…"

"What you heard?"

"Yeah."

I could see her gather up her courage, and stick it into place. Ellen doubted herself, but I knew better. Guts of steel and nerves of whipcord, even if she didn't know it yet. Like any rookie, she had to learn.

"What is it?" she asked.

"Fatae."

"I figured that out already," she said, her voice terse. I shouldn't screw with her, not when it came to her visions. Most Talent I know, they're happy to be what they are. Ellen, burdened with the extra "gift" of being a storm-seer, wasn't there yet. She would be, eventually. There was too much that was glorious in magic for her to resist it, even I knew that. But not yet.

143

We crested the hill, and had a choice of paths, when the one we were on branched. The left-hand choice went back down the hill at a slant. The right-hand choice turned into a series of steps, and led not into the valley, but to a rocky alcove set in the hill, complete with benches carved out of the rock. It was pretty, but not where we were going.

"Left," I said, but Ellen was already heading down the path. Her rough-tread hiking boots were better for this than my cowboy boots. I should have changed before we came out here, but neither of us had wanted to take the time to go back to the office, much less my apartment uptown. The trip out here was a pain on mass transit, and I wanted to get here before night.

Not that I hadn't spent time in cemeteries at night, but never willingly, and this one... this one had a reputation. Both good and not-good.

The noise got louder, as we went down the hill. It wasn't loud, in and of itself; you wouldn't have heard it if there was heavy traffic. It was like walking under a tree full of chattering birds, except it was coming from ground level, and it sounded...worse.

I should have warned Ellen, but how the hell do you prep someone for this?

"Ack!" She jumped back, damn near into my arms, and I caught her as gently as I could. "Steady..."

The figure in front of us was about four feet tall, and barely a foot wide, and looked a hell of a lot like a bulked-up preying mantis, if preying mantis' had unnervingly human faces behind the mandibles. Exactly who I'd hoped to run into.

It clicked at us, and tilted its head.

"Sorry to interrupt you," I started to say, but those pop-set black eyes looked past me, right at Ellen, and chittered at her. I turned to look, just in time to see her shock slide back behind her usual poker face. Good girl, you don't ever let them see you be shook.

"You are not dead," it said, almost accusingly. "Only the dead come to us."

"We are not dead," I agreed. "But we have an interest in the dead. Not the same interest you have," I hurried to clarify, just in case it thought we were competition. "Only in knowing if you have recently…" encountered? Eaten? "If anyone new has been brought to your attention."

"There are always new, always old." It couldn't seem to stop staring at Ellen, which was making both of us uneasy. I realized that there were others gathering, a few feet away. All right, I'd known they would be in a pack, or whatever they called themselves, but knowing that and seeing it up close and personal was a bit much. Normally I could handle anything the city threw at me with a certain level of calm, but this… These things would strip the flesh from my bones, when my time came, and crunch the bones into dust. It was what they did, it was their purpose in the circle of fucking life, but I hadn't expected to ever actually face it while still breathing.

"These would be…two men," I managed to say, keeping what I thought—hoped—was a calm, cool note in my voice. "Humans. One black, one white?" I had no idea if it could even differentiate, with those eyes. "Still alive."

"The living do not interest us." Its gaze was still stuck past my shoulder.

"Yeah. Could have fooled me about that." I shifted so that Ellen was entirely behind me, and tried to catch its attention again. "If you saw these men, would you tell me about it?"

"If you came and asked me after I had seen them."

Took me a second to puzzle that one out, and I suspected that was as good as I was going to get. Doubtful they'd have access to telephones, much less the internet, and none of them were going to leave the grounds. Specifically, they *couldn't* leave the grounds.

145

Old story, of which I knew only the base legend: turf war; they lost.

I didn't bother to say thank you: carrion-eaters weren't notorious for their adherence to Ms. Manners' finest, and I wanted to get Ellen—and myself—away from them soonest possible.

The slope back up seemed steeper than it had coming down, and neither of us stopped to talk until we were at the ridge again, and then back over the other side.

"The *hell?*"

I flinched. My mother used to have that same tone of voice: not shouting, but strong enough to break a ten-year-old's nerve. "They're called Direlings. They're categorized as mostly harmless."

"Unless you happen to be dead. Or me. That thing wanted to touch me. What is it with fatae trying to *touch* me?"

"It's all that current you have coiled inside you," I said, remembering my informant down the seaport, who had wanted very badly to touch my Shadow, too. I couldn't think of any others, offhand, but she sounded like there had been a few. I frowned. I'd never felt any urge to touch her, not like that, but... I spent a considerable about of time around Talent, and I knew better. If Valere didn't chop my hand off, Bonnie would. "They—we—can feel it, like electricity on our skin. And some of 'em," and I looked over my shoulder, an instinctive gesture, to make sure nobody was following us. "Some of 'em are just damned creepy."

"Yeah creepy as fuck. You take me to all the best places, boss. I want to go home and take a long, hot shower. With a scrub brush."

We caught the subway just as it pulled into the station, slipping into a half-full car as far away from a noisy bunch of teenagers as we—and the other adults in the car—could manage. It had been a long day, and Ellen had done well, but there was something in her eyes that I didn't think was just because she'd gotten ooked out by the direlings. Or not only because. I kept silent the first few stops, then leaned into her personal space just enough that we could keep the conversations semi-private.

"The guys you saw, they were alive. And you heard the sound when they were still alive. So whatever was going to happen to them, it happens there. Direlings have no reason to hurt the living, so maybe now that they're aware of it–"

Ellen stared at one of the ads telling us in English and Spanish that the only way to get ahead was to learn radiology skills. "Do you really think those things will stop someone getting killed? Why should they interrupt someone giving them more to eat?"

"Shadow, you know how many fatae die every day in the city? No direling has ever gone hungry." All right, maybe that wasn't the best thing to think about. I gripped the pole and let myself sway with the movement of the subway car as we pulled out of Brooklyn and headed under the river to Manhattan. "You need to trust your instincts." This was an on-going argument: she trusted her instincts about as much as I trusted the Mayor's office. That is to say, we trusted them to screw it up.

"Okay, you need to trust me that I trust your instincts. How's that?" It felt like dirty pool, and not what I was supposed to be teaching her, but if it got that look out of her eyes, I could let her go home to that much-needed hot shower and hopefully a decent night's sleep.

The train curved around a corner and she got a minute as everyone shifted to adjust before having to answer.

"Okay?" I was pushing. I could hear myself pushing. Ellen was starting to turn into a solid investigator: she had an eye for details, the ability to think on her feet, and a deep-seated suspicion of everyone's story. But she doubted her own, too, and that was a problem.

Most PIs are assholes not because we're assholes, but because we've learned that the only thing we can trust us our own gut. And the gut, as my old partner used to say, is directly connected to the asshole. Ellen still tried to please and placate as a way to stay off everyone's radar. I should be pushing her to fight me, to stand her ground… but not today.

"All right," she said finally. "Yeah." And then with a little more certainty, "Yeah, you're right. But what are we supposed to do? I mean we can't stake out the cemetery, not and follow up on the case, too." She tilted her head at me, and I was struck again by the lines of her face. Most young women would be self-conscious about that strong a nose and jawline, but Ellen didn't seem to even notice. Cleopatra herself would have been proud. Now to get the rest of her to follow suit…

"I don't know, kid. That's why we only take one client at a time. You can't spread yourself thin and expect to make a real difference." It wasn't a consoling thing to say, but if I'd bullshitted her here, she'd know. She'd heard me talk about focus often enough before.

"My visions are—"

"Your visions are important." I headed that one off at the pass, before she started to wonder about a certain double-headed coin in my pocket. "If we need to call in help to cover all the corners, we will. It's not like we're alone in this. The PUPS would love to have a chance to out-spook the spooks, given a chance." I grinned at her, and she smiled, reluctantly, back. Venec would hop at the chance to train some of his newbies, at our expense.

We split at South Ferry, me heading back uptown, her off to the tiny apartment she'd gotten in the East Village. It was about the size of my bathroom, but the building was solid—both Didier and I had checked it out—and the landlord wasn't on any of the NYPD slumlists, so it was about as good as an underemployed twenty-something without a trust fund was going to get, without leaving the island, and Valere had been clear that she was to stay within reach. The mentor-mentee thing used to involve fostering as well, I'd been told, but Ellen's case was slightly beyond that, considering her age.

It was funny, really. To look at us, you'd think there was only about a decade's difference. She'd had to grow up fast, and I'd... well, fauns age slower than humans. My hair was still dark and my bones didn't creak, but there were days I felt older than dirt. Today—staring a carrion-eater in the mandibles—I felt every grain of it.

Ellen slogged her way up the three flights of stairs to her apartment, unlocked the door, and fell inside, shedding clothes as she went. She hadn't been joking, entirely, about needing that shower. The way the direling had looked at her, its hand-claw-things opening and shutting like it wanted to measure the density of her bones just before it crunched into her...ugh.

It wouldn't have touched her. Danny wouldn't have let it. Her boss might come across as being sort of laconic, maybe a little slow, with the way his body slouched and especially when he pulled the baseball cap down low over his face, but she knew that there was muscle under that jacket, and an inhuman strength that could throw a full-grown human off it tracks without breaking a sweat. Plus, he had the seriously overprotective thing going on, even when he tried not to let it show.

Genevieve had warned her about that, months ago. "Danny's a good guy. But he's got...a thing."

"About women?"

"About throwaways." Her mentor was a lot of things, but subtle wasn't one of them. That was why she left negotiations to her partner. "He wants to save the world, especially the underage part of the world."

"I'm not underage." She hadn't been, mentally, since she was

149

around twelve, and started seeing things out of the corner of her eye, making her parents think she was crazy. Since she'd manifested as a Talent, on a family that didn't have a clue magic existed.

"You know what I mean." Genevieve had given her that Look, the one that said she'd expected better, smarter, from her mentee, and that had been the end of that conversation.

The shower was hot, almost to the point of scalding, and at this hour of the evening, when most people were just heading home or making dinner, there was actual water pressure. Ellen would have been content to stay there for an hour, except that ten minutes was about as long as she could count on the water staying hot.

She debating washing her hair, and then decided it didn't need it yet, and she really didn't have the patience needed to deal with it, after. Pulling on sweats, and tossing her day's clothing into the hamper, Ellen curled up on the sofa on her living room/dining room/work area, and reached for her notebook.

Danny had done his Q&A, right after the vision, because he thought the first reactions were the best, the clearest. Ellen didn't disagree, exactly, but she was starting to think that what lingered was important, too. Like in a dream, the details that sunk in and stayed were often pointing toward the thing you needed to remember. Or what might trigger an understanding of the dream.

She shivered, and pulled a blanket up over her legs, even though the apartment was a reasonable temperature. The problem with that theory was that visions weren't dreams. They didn't come from her subconscious, but someone else's energy, getting caught up in the current and arrowing in to her. They called her a storm-seer because storms picked up and tossed current around like whoa, and she caught the brunt of that every time, but once she'd gotten a little of her own current stored, the visions started finding her whenever there was the slightest surge.

Most of them were small twinges, a sense of something being wrong, but not enough information to act on. Enough to wake her up in the night, but not enough to tell anyone about. She held the fragments close, and tried to remember what she could, knowing that she might be the only person in the world to know that someone was in danger.

She couldn't control them, that was the problem. She couldn't close the door and say "sorry, busy." Danny had taken her in to make use of those visions—both Genevieve and Bonnie were right, he couldn't say no to someone in need—but she was distracting him from someone else who needed help, now.

That…sucked. That more than sucked.

And yeah, they could get one of the Pups to stake out the place—stake out a cemetery, ok the jokes just wrote themselves—but that felt wrong to her. Not that they wouldn't do a fine job but…the visions came to her. She was the one supposed to do something about them. It was her responsibility.

"Tomorrow, we need to be focusing on Mister McConnell," she said, staring down at her open notebook. "Danny shouldn't be stressing over this, too."

So what did she have? The vision had been quiet, except for the chittering noise. And not-bright. Not dark, exactly, not like it would have been at night, but red-shadowed, like…dawn.

She knew where, and now she knew when. She just didn't know who, or why.

Only the who mattered.

She was off the couch and pulling a clean pair of jeans out of the drawer before she realized that she'd made a decision.

And she wasn't going to call Danny. This was her deal. She was going to watch, and shout an alarm, and that was all. Let the boss sleep.

6

Despite the urgent feeling driving her, Ellen was smart enough—despite what some people thought—not to just rush out to the cemetery, especially at night. She dressed carefully in layers, so that she wouldn't get cold while she was waiting, and brewed a thermos of coffee to take with her. She packed that in a backpack from her days living in Central Park, threw in the leftover half of a deli sandwich from the day before, and a pear, just in case she got hungry, then reconsidered and added a chocolate bar, too. She'd been hoarding it for a bad day, but she thought sitting on cold grass all night waiting to see if someone got killed, qualified.

Her mother's voice sifted through the back of her head where she usually kept it locked down, reminding her that sitting on cold grass all night wasn't required. Her mother had been not the best mother in the world, maybe, but it hadn't been because she was a stupid woman. Ellen went into her closet and pulled out the folding beach chair she'd bought on the off chance that she might have a day she wanted to go to Coney Island or something, and put that by the door, too. Collapsed into its carrying case, it was small profile enough she shouldn't get too many dirty looks.

In fact, she did get looks, but mainly because she caught the tail end of rush hour, and there wasn't really enough room for both her backpack and the collapsed chair, crushed in with so many other people. She made herself as small and unimposing as possible, but she wasn't Genevieve, who could make herself disappear even when you were looking at her. Ellen was tall, with broad shoulders and sharp features, and people *saw* her, even when she didn't want them to. Especially when she didn't want them to.

Slowly, the train emptied out as they got further into Brooklyn, and Ellen was able to exhale slightly, letting her shoulders slump. Genevieve was always telling her to listen to the subway cars, feel the current running with them, and learn how to pick up a little of that, siphoning it off in a slow but steady trickle. It was hard to find it, though, when there were so many other people around. She couldn't relax enough to feel it, wasn't comfortable opening her own core to take it in. But she hadn't done a full charge in a while, and her mentor hammered into her head enough times that the moment you ran down was when you'd need to pull up something massive. Ellen had the advantage over most other Talent for being able to find and use ley lines easily, but you couldn't count on there being a line within reach. So: trickle charge, whenever and wherever she could.

Grabbing an open seat, Ellen set her bags between her knees for safety, leaned her head back and closed her eyes, trying to feel the thrum of current sliding around her. It was faint, like a dry tickle in her throat, but she found it, touched it. Her breathing slowed, and she tried to remember what Genevieve had taught her. Find, touch. Open. Everyone visualized it differently, everyone handled it differently. In Ellen's mind, her core was like her mother's yarn stash, if the yarn were alive. Different colors, different textures, mostly either wrapped in a skein or coiled in a ball. It was hard to

153

imagine closing or opening it the way Genevieve talked about, but she could unwind it, slip the end of the new current in, and rewind it into the appropriate skein…

Distracted by what she was about to do, worried about how she was going to sneak into the cemetery, and what she might face, thinking that she should have packed something that could act like a weapon, Ellen almost didn't notice when the first thread of train-current wound itself into her hands, and her hands automatically fed it into the existing ball of current, and it wound itself around and curled up inside her core like a contented cat.

"Huh," she said, once she realized what had happened. She didn't feel any different, but there was a sense of…well-being that trumped her worries, just for an instant. "Not bad. Not bad at all." By the time they reached her stop, Ellen was humming under her breath, and as she left the train, she patted it once, like saying thank you.

Aboveground, night had already descended. She walked toward the gate, trying to remember everything Genevieve had ever told her about no-see-mees, the cantrip she used to keep people from seeing her. Her mentor was a natural Retriever; the cantrip merely enhanced her skills. Ellen would be starting from the opposite end.

"On the plus side, I already have an advantage she doesn't," Ellen said, amused despite herself. Genevieve was smart and skilled, and white. Being black couldn't be called an advantage most days, but paler skin would be more visible, if a guard were patrolling.

In the end, though, it was anticlimactic: there were no guards, and the wrought-iron gates closing the arch were designed to keep cars out, not people. Ellen slipped between the gates without too much trouble, then pulled her bags through after her.

It took her seeming forever to find the path Danny had led them along, but there were signs at the intersections of the roads, just like real streets, and the hill they'd climbed was marked by a squat marble tomb with a marble cat perched on the roof. She paused at the ridge, squatting down so that she didn't stand out if anyone where looking that way, and considered her options.

There was no way that she could patrol the entire cemetery—it was huge. But she didn't need to: Danny had said that the direful, direlings, whatever, mostly stayed in one place, where the city's fatae were taken to be disposed of. So the guys in her vision would have to be there, if she'd heard that much of their noise. But what-

"Hey, Ellen."

Ellen turned, still squatting, and almost busted up her knee, crying out on shock and pain.

"Whoa, hey, sorry," and hands caught her, helping her up. The other person squatted next to her. Male, slender build, pale skin smudged with dirt, a black watch cap pulled down low over his forehead, and eyes....

Calm gray eyes that she knew. "Damn it, Pietr." She sat down hard on the grass and stared up at one of the senior PUps. "What the hell are you doing here?" She kept her voice low, so it wouldn't carry, but shoved as much annoyance into the words as she could manage, to irritated and embarrassed to be afraid.

"Your boss asked us to keep an eye on the place tonight. He didn't send you?"

"No." She glared at him, then relented. He hadn't meant to spook her like that, probably. And Danny... the boss could be a bastard sometimes, but it was so like him to do this. Like the two-sided coin he thought she hadn't figure out yet. "It's not his case," she said. "It's mine."

Pietr had been there when she'd first learned what she was. He'd understand what she meant.

"Oh. Huh. Okay, you're the boss, then. What're we looking for?"

"Two men. One's black, I'm pretty sure the other one's white, but he might be Asian. Same height, broad-shouldered. I didn't see their faces."

"And they're coming here, why? I mean, generally the only folk who come here are dead folk, people burying dead folk, and people planning to unbury dead folk. Different bait needed for all three."

"Your world is a terrifying place," she told him.

"Yeah." Pietr didn't smile, but she heard the humor in his voice. "Yeah, it is."

Pietr approved of her chair, his muttered "Wish I'd thought of that" giving her a brief glow of satisfaction. He had scouted the area before she arrived, and determined that the rocky ledge on the left hand path actually had a nice overlook of the slope, and the area where the direlings gathered. "If that's where you think the guy will come, then that's where we should scope out."

And by "we" he meant her. Pietr disappeared into the shadows, almost as easily as Genevieve did. His plan was to go closer, make sure that they didn't miss anything. "If anything happens— anything at all, you hear me? Ping. I'll be there in a blink."

From anyone else she might have thought that meant he'd come running, but Piet was a Pup and that meant he'd probably learned to Translocate pretty well, especially after he'd taken a good look around her location, practically memorizing the space.

Ellen might have felt slighted, put in an observer's position, but she was just as thankful to not get any closer to the carrion-eaters than she had to. It wasn't only the way their leader had looked at her, there was something about their smell that made her uneasy, as though her visions had somehow tainted her, made her smell like death, too.

She settled into her chair, pulled out the thermos of coffee, and lifted Pietr's binocs to her eyes, scanning the slight valley below.

Nothing happened. Ellen let her senses open as wide as she could, the way Genevieve taught her, but there didn't seem to be any current moving at all; she couldn't even sense Pietr. Her legs went to sleep, and she got up to pace, waking them from pins and needles. She got bored, and reached for the nearest ley line, finding it a few miles to the north. She wondered what would happen if they built a cemetery over a ley line and decided that's when you got zombies. She did a few yoga moves, then went back to her chair, suddenly worried that she'd missed something.

"Midnight."

Ellen jumped out of her chair, turning in the direction of the voice. A huge black bird was perched on the stone bench, staring at her. Ellen blinked, slightly nervous. The thing was huge, with a wicked beak, and it was staring at her, way too intently. Like she was dinner.

"Did you say that?" she asked.

The bird—a raven, she thought, or the biggest damned crow she'd ever seen—shifted on its legs, back and forth, and kept staring at her, not saying anything.

"It's not midnight, bird," she said finally. "It's got to be closer to 3am." She hoped, anyway. The thought of having to sit here another five hours made her want to cry.

The bird made a noise that wasn't words, but Ellen thought uncomfortably might have been a laugh, like it knew what she was thinking. "Look underneath," it said, and then spread those huge wings and flapped off, disappearing into the darkness.

"What?" She didn't know if she was asking the now-departed bird, or the dead around her, or a God she wasn't sure was paying attention any more. Either way, she didn't get an answer.

The coffee had gotten cold and bitter, but Ellen drank it anyway. She thought about pinging Pietr, but decided that she'd sound like a spooked kid if she did so.

"So, a talking raven. Happens all the time in New York," she said, trying to mimic Pietr and failing miserably. She thought she sounded more like Sergei with a head cold. "So yeah, a talking raven. Who said midnight, maybe, and look underneath, probably."

No, definitely. She hadn't been paying attention when the first noise came, but she'd been listening, the second time.

Ravens talked, she knew that much. Or, they could mimic words. Did the words actually mean anything? Once, she would have assumed it was a hallucination, just another bit of proof that she was crazy, her brain constantly playing tricks on her.

The fatae existed. Talking, advice-giving ravens? Not so much a stretch, after that. But did it *mean* anything?

"Coincidences happen." That had been one of the first lessons Danny had given her. He meant that sometimes you could look so hard to find a connection, trying to solve a case, that you forgot that the universe was random, and sometimes shit just happened. No deeper meaning or pattern, or at least, none that was relevant to the question at hand. On the other hand, it wasn't as though she had anything else to do, just then.

"Look underneath what? Under the ground?" They were in a cemetery, so that would make sense, she supposed. "Under the skin? Ugh. Under the hat? Undertow?" She picked up the binocs and went back to searching the landscape. "Stupid bird. What was wrong with "nevermore,"anyway?"

almost dawn. looks like tonight was a bust

Pietr's ping was as stealthy as he was: she barely realized it was someone else's impression in her head, not just her thinking the same thing.

the light was iffy in my vision she sent back, not so much the words as the memory of the vision. *not giving up until the sun's up*

158

fair enough a sense of understanding, and a hint of a salute. Ellen shook her head: Pups took orders from no-one except their boss, Benjamin Venec, and not always even then, from the stories she'd heard. Genevieve admitted that she wasn't sure what to make of the Pups—they were the only ones who'd ever been able to track her down, even if they hadn't been able to stop her, and that colored her opinion—but Ellen liked them. Bonnie had been the one to step in, when Ellen fell in with the wrong crowd, and who had matched her with Genevieve, and if it was Bonnie and the other pups who'd also shown her what she was, what her visions meant… well, it was better than being scared she was losing her mind, wasn't it?

That thought tickled another one, some connection or correlation. Ellen looked again through the binocs, then rested her eyes for a moment, and looked again. The thought slid closer, almost within reach, and the vision unfolded in her memory, as delicate as dandelion fluff and just as likely to blow away if she disturbed it.

Two men, black and white. Same build, same height, same…

Same.

Losing her mind. Twins? Look underneath.

She tucked the binocs into her backpack and slung it over her shoulder, but left the chair behind as she moved down the stairs, down the left-hand path, following some instinct: no, not even an instinct, a whisper of a thought. She knew she should ping Pietr, tell him where she was going, but she didn't know, and even the second it took to form the ping and send it might lose that whisper.

She followed the path mainly by the sense of *rightness* drawing her, since this area of the cemetery was dimly-lit, at best. Bushes rustled and things crackled, but Ellen summoned a thread of current and let it glimmer under her skin, and whatever it was decided to leave her alone.

159

She heard the chittering off to the left. Whatever was drawing her was drawing them, too. Ellen looked up. The light was shifting, just like in her vision. The clouds had cleared and the moon was bright on the horizon, even as the faintest pink was starting to creep into the eastern sky. Up ahead there was the glint of water, and her breath caught.

"Here and now," she whispered, and finally paused long enough to ping Pietr

here and now and a sense of the water in front of her, a single huge tree just ahead, the path curving to the right, even as she was walking faster, and then running.

Not two men. One. He was cast in shadows, standing by the water. Too-close, Ellen could see-sense—the presence of direlings. Not approaching; waiting. Ghouls at the feast-to-be. The chittering was faint but she could hear it, raising the hair on her arms.

"They don't eat the living," she reminded herself. Where the hell was Pietr?

"Hey." She spoke softly, the way she used to when she lived back home and was never sure what kind of reception she'd get, what she'd done to piss people off this time. One guy, wrapped in shadows, his posture broad-shouldered yeah but somehow slumped in on himself. She exhaled, and counted back from three into magesight, trying to find out what about this guy drew her.

Human—a Null, without magic—but there was something funky about him. His silhouette wouldn't stay tight, shifting from a normal misty-black to this intensely annoying glimmer, too harsh to look at directly, like staring at the sun. He moved, and the double-image moved too, like…

Like two men, not black and white but sharp and muted. She didn't know why or how, but there were two of him in the one. Her mind flitted through a race of ideas, discarding them almost as

160

quickly. Possession was a myth, ghosts were rare, and chimeras manifested outwardly, not like this.

"Go away."

His voice was low, too, but not soft. The shifting sharpness she saw was in his voice, scraping at the air.

"Can't do that. What's wrong?"

"Everything. Nothing." His edges almost connected, then shifted apart again. Ellen was having trouble keeping track of the magesight and the conversation, but was afraid to let go of either. "I'm just too tired to keep it together, that's all. Why do you care?"

She swallowed. Where the *hell* was Pietr? "Because I do. This... this isn't the answer." She didn't know how he was thinking he'd kill himself; the pond couldn't be all that deep. But it was clear that was what he was planning. "It's really not."

There was a tingle of current, like a flash through the air, and she heard obvious footsteps behind her. Pietr, finally. *this is him* she pinged. *i don't know what to do*

he's alive Reassurance and reminder: whatever was going to happen hadn't, yet. She was in time. But could she *do* anything? "Please."

"I'm tired," he said. "Tired and crazy and why the hell were you even here? Nobody here except us dead men."

The chittering in the distance go louder, as though his words made them anticipate. *Fuck you* she thought, fiercely desperate. *You don't get him yet.*

"It's my choice."

She looked at Pietr, but he'd taken a step back, and she knew he wouldn't interfere. It was up to her.

"I saw you. That means you're supposed to live."

"What the hell does that mean?" His outline shimmered and almost clicked, then fractured into painful sunspots again.

wildly bi-polar Pietr pinged, the actual thought like a

161

lightning flash in her brain. *or split personalities? Something that's causing him enough pain he can't handle it*

"You can get help. There're doctors, medications…"

The stranger's voice held an undercurrent of savage laughter that unnerved her almost as much as the direlings gossiping to themselves behind them. "You don't know that. You think I haven't *tried?*"

"You're not crazy." He was, he absolutely was, but she'd thought she was crazy too, probably was crazy, after everything, after getting dying people shoved into her head, and she wasn't sure what the hell crazy meant any more. "No more than anyone else. Don't do this. You're supposed to live."

"You're as crazy as I am. You don't know that."

No, she didn't. Too many she Saw were dead already. But not this one. Not yet.

"It's your choice," Pietr said quietly, "but you don't know she's not right."

"Not today," Ellen said. "Not this way. Not face down in a pond, stripped to your bones by carrion-eaters. Do you hear them? They're waiting for you. They won't even give you the decency of a proper burial. Screw them. Walk away." She shoved every certainty she had into her voice, and prayed it would be enough. "I wouldn't have stayed out here all night, freezing my ass off, if you weren't supposed to walk away, after. *Alive.*"

"All night? Why the hell were you sitting here all night?" He turned, and she could see, in the growing graying light, that he was older than she'd thought, maybe even in his fifties, and the expression on his face was one of disbelief, and—worry?

"So I could be here when you needed me," she said, as though it were the most obvious thing in the world. And right then, to her, it was.

"Fuck." He turned back to look at the water, and she let go of

162

the mage-sight, knowing somehow that she'd won, that he wouldn't do anything now.

"Go the fuck away," he said. She nodded, then turned and walked away. He'd done as she'd asked, she could do as he'd asked.

Pietr and Ellen walked back up the path to where she'd left her chair, then turned to look again, the light enough to see clearly, now. He was still standing there by the edge of the water, a rough shadow, but as they watched, he turned and walked away.

"He's someone's dad," Pietr said. "Probably a daughter. He wouldn't—couldn't—do anything while you were there."

"He could still do it again tomorrow," she said.

"He could. It's his choice. But you gave him something to think about today. You gave him someone who cared."

She wouldn't see the sharp-and-muted man again; the visions didn't work like that. At least, she didn't think so. She'd never know what happened to him, because she didn't think he'd be dumb enough to come here again, to try.

She'd won. For this one moment, she won.

"C'mon, kid," Pietr said, even though he couldn't be all that much older than her. "Let's get the hell out of here. I'll buy you a cup of coffee."

Coffee. She didn't drink the stuff, but she needed to pick up a new coffee maker for the office. And take a shower. And get to the office. And...

Yeah," she said, folding up the chair and shoving it into the carry-bag. "Getting out of here sounds good."

7

"Jesus. Look what the cat wouldn't bother dragging in." I'd seen Ellen tired before—we'd worked some insane hours—but this took the proverbial cake, and a cupcake beside. "I hope you left the other person or persons in similar shape?"

She put a brown shopping bag on the desk, and tried to glare at me, but a yawn caught her off-guard. She'd tied a bright blue scarf around her hair. I liked it. It made her seem funkier, younger.

"And you're late," I went on, knowing better than to comment on her attire, at least. I made a show of looking at my watch, a clunky wind-up that had survived more than a decade of working around Talent.

"Yeah well, I got us a new coffee machine," she said, indicating the bag. "And I solved the vision."

"Oh, good," I said, although I'd actually made a pot at home, before heading in, and filled a thermos. "And wait, you did what?" I squinted at her. "Shadow, tell me you didn't go back to the cemetery last night."

"Okay." She started to unpack the bag, taking out what looked like a basic but shiny espresso machine. Well, that would be classier than our old Mister Coffee, for sure.

"Okay you didn't, or okay you won't tell me?" Jesus, I was starting to sound like my mother. Although there were worse people to sound like, given the situation. "You went back to the cemetery." I wanted to yell at her but despite all sound-alikes, I wasn't her mother, and the visions were hers, not mine.

"Pietr was there," she said, heading off my next question. "So it wasn't like I was alone."

She hadn't known he'd be there when she went, though. I decided not to push it. Instead, I took the bits and pieces of the coffee maker out of her hands, and started assembling them on the counter. "So tell me what happened."

She told me, complete with shifty-eyed looks when she left something out, and expressive hand gestures I didn't think she was even aware she was making. Normally she kept her body still and quiet when she spoke, as though afraid to attract attention, or like someone had told her it was impolite to fill the air outside your own personal space.

"I'm still pissed that you went back out there without arranging for backup," I said when she was done. "That was incredibly stupid." Even when I was working alone, if I was going into a potentially hazardous situation, I called for help. Most of the time. Enough that I felt justified scolding her. "But you did good. I'm proud of you. And no, you're not getting a raise. Like you pointed out, this was your gig, your time."

I fitted the last piece of the machine together and frowned at it. We'd need better coffee, to go with this thing.

"And now we're back on the clock with the McConnell case. You going to be able to stay awake?"

I turned back just in time to see her pull a two-liter bottle of Dr. Pepper from the shopping bag. Question answered.

"So, what's on the agenda?"

She was being far too cheerful. If someone else had come in and announced that they'd stayed up all night and cracked the case, I'd expect more than a little ego-puffing and outward satisfaction. But I was starting to figure my Shadow out, a bit. She had an ingrown sense of responsibility for shit that wasn't her fault, and when it was her responsibility she went a little overboard. So yeah, she cracked the case, but she'd only saved the guy once, and he sounded like there was way more than walking off the ledge to be done. She was smart enough to know that, too.

But if she was going to pretend she wasn't thinking about that, I was willing to let it go. My promise had been to teach her, and help her find the people in her visions, that was all. Knowing that she was repressing the worry…well, indulging in the worry, wasn't much better. To each their own emotional management techniques.

"We need to follow up on the most viable leads, which would be the possible connection between our missing man, and the possible offspring. So it's time to visit mom. Or mom's people, anyway."

That got her attention. Ellen had spent the past ten years being told that the not-humans she thought she saw weren't real, and she was still torn between fascination and unease around the fatae—at least, new breeds. She was used to me by now, and PB was so overt you almost forgot about him. Demon were like that.

"How do you know what she is—or who she is? The report Mahiba gave us only had a name."

"Names are chock full of information, if you know what you're looking for," I told her, picking up my coat and waiting for her to do the same before escorting her out and locking the door. She added a quick cantrip to seal the lock—I never bothered before but it made her feel better, and was good practice.

166

And a little extra protection never hurt anyone.

"Names?" she prompted.

"Right. It's like human cultures, where different names are popular at different times, and in different countries. You won't find many guys named Jesus in Scandinavia, for example, or women named Mary-Margaret in Jewish families, right?"

"Not unless they married in. But yeah, okay. So what does "Kerrieon" tell you?"

I paused outside the elevator, and sighed. "Lilin."

Some of the breeds prefer to live alone, mingling more with outsiders than their own kin and kind. Others gathered in enclaves, usually somewhere like Central Park, or—in the case of some of our less social types—in the tunnels below the subways. The Lilin, not unexpectedly, went upscale. Their enclave was out in one of the better neighborhoods of Brooklyn, in a pre-war building that had clearly been updated to modern standards while still retaining the charm of the original. Say what you will about Lilin, and history certainly wasn't quiet, they had style and taste.

The rain had cleared, but it was still damp and miserable outside. We found a place to park the rental car a few blocks away, and walked down the street in silence. There had been discussions about how to approach this, but none of them had seemed guaranteed to win friends and influence confessions. We walked up the brownstone's steps without a clue how we were going to proceed. Not that something like that had ever stopped me.

"Well, hello."

The woman who opened the door was wearing jeans and a heavy sweater than hit her mid-hip. She was in her early fifties, at a rough visual, with blond hair cut short, and faint wrinkles around the eyes. Her voice didn't ooze sensuality, and she wasn't particularly va-voom, but every part of my body stood up and took notice. It wasn't personal on either side, so we both pretended it wasn't happening.

"We need to speak with your elders," I said, giving the courtesy of assuming that wasn't her. She didn't blink or show any sign of surprise, but stepped back into the hallway and let us come in.

"May I take your coats?" she asked. "You'll need to wait a bit, before they are able to see you."

We handed over our jackets, and let ourselves be escorted into the parlor on the first floor. It was a comfortable room, cozy in a way that made you expect to see a cat draped over one of the sofas, and a paperback book left on the end-table, half-read. There was in fact a cat, opening one sleepy eye to assess us and then going back to sleep, but the end-table held a series of cell phones and an e-reader, instead. The fatae had adapted quite easily to the technological age, thank you very much.

Ellen sat down next to the cat, who deigned to uncurl and let itself be scratched behind the ears. It blinked at me, and I blinked back from my chair on the opposite side of the grouping. I like cats fine, but I could see the door from my position, and that was more important to me. We waited a few minutes, maybe ten, max, and then the door swung open again and two Lilin walked in.

The woman at the door had been sexy. These two were seduction personified. I regretted letting Ellen come with me, even though I knew it was better that she encounter them first with me to look out for her. Despite whatever you've heard about succubi or incubi, Lilin don't intentionally go out to seduce mortals. In fact, most of the time they don't even crook a finger. They just happen to be deeply sexual beings, and human chemicals respond to that.

So do most fatae, if we're being honest, and faun genetics are predisposed to anything that sparks of a good time. I ignored my dick with the poise of years of practice, and offered my hand in greeting to the elders.

"Thank you for your time, so unexpectedly," I said. "My name is Daniel Hendrickson, this is my associate, Ellen." She had refused to give or use her last name—given her family history, I could understand that—so I went traditional. "Ellen *Ychna bat* Genevieve." I handed the woman my card, and she took it with grave, graceful formality.

"I am Alineon Layil," she said. "This is my brother Simeon. How may we aid you?" She gestured for us both to be seated again, and took chairs of their own. The cat climbed back into Ellen's lap and went to sleep.

"It is in the matter of Kerrieon Lavil," I said. "And her infant."

"Infant?" That got Simeon's attention; he sat up out of his previously indolent drape, and leaned forward, intent as a mouser spotting movement. "Kerrieon had no infant."

"Simi. Pause and let the faun speak."

"She is on record as having given birth nearly nine months ago. To a half-human child." All right, we didn't know that for certain—there were no medical records. But she'd named a human as father, so that was what we were going on.

"Impossible," Alice retorted.

Hardly impossible, with me here as witness. I didn't say that, though. "Is the girl here to speak for herself?"

"No." The woman didn't flinch from my question. "She has not lived here in several months."

"A year," Simeon said. "If the laundry comes out, at least let it all come out. She left us a year ago."

"And went where?"

"We don't know. What happened to the infant, Mister Hendrickson?"

"We were hoping that you could tell us that."

"No. As I said, we did not even know that she was pregnant. Had we–"

169

"You seemed taken aback that she gave birth to a cross-breed."

That caused Simeon to let out a bark of laughter that wasn't even remotely amused. "Taken aback, yes. But—no. I see where your thoughts go and no. Never. We would have taken the infant in, no matter its parentage"

I believed them. Like I'd told Ellen, babies are rare enough. And it wasn't as though Lilin hadn't proven they were cross-fertile, millennia ago. Rare, but not impossible. They'd been reacting to the fact of their not-knowing, not the impossibility of the act, then.

"Does she have friends here?" Ellen spoke up for the first time, one hand still petting the cat. "Sisters? Best-friends-forever kind of friends, that she would have confided in?"

"Rachel, perhaps. A human girl she went to school with. But Kerrieon was not the sort to confide. She was…" Alice paused, and my bullshit detector gave a faint tremor. "She was not a girl prone to belonging, if you understand my meaning."

Ellen raised her eyebrows, and I almost laughed. Of all the *Cosa* members in this city, they were talking to two people who could *absolutely* understand that.

"Do you think she's all right?" Simeon said. "Both of them—the baby and Kerrieon ?"

"That's what we're trying to find out, sir."

"If there's anything we can do to help, please let us know. And if you find the infant…" He looked to Alineon for permission, first, and when she nodded faintly, went on "it will have a home here. If it's needed."

The infant, not the mother. Interesting.

"Oh *god*." Ellen barely held her reaction to the Lilin until the door closed behind them and they were back on the street. Danny laughed a little—at her, she thought. But fair enough.

170

"Yeah," he said. "They're a bit much, aren't they."

"Are they succubi? I mean, succubi and incubi?"

"Ugly nicknames for a perfectly respectable breed," he said. "Don't use those terms in polite company. That was good thinking about the boon companion. Do you think they were lying?"

"Yes," she said without hesitation. "Or, they think there might be someone, and they didn't want us talking to her. Or him."

"To what purpose?"

Danny did that, asked questions in the middle of a job, made her say what she was thinking, verbalize her thoughts no matter how dumb they sounded. Sergei laughed when she'd complained, said Danny was making her self-actualize, whatever that meant. But he was right: if there was a flaw in her logic, it was more obvious when she said it out loud.

"Because they want to deal with it themselves. They live all together, you said, so they probably aren't used to trusting outsiders… if someone screwed up and a member—and a baby—disappeared, they're going to want to handle it internally."

"Reasonable." They had reached the car, and Ellen scanned the windshield for a ticket. There was none, so she unlocked the door and got in, waiting while Danny got in on the passenger side. "And also reasonable to assume that they did not take the baby, since they didn't know about it. Unless they're playing a very deep game to throw us off their tracks but that's unlikely. Most people just aren't that complicated, and too many people in that house would have to know about it, and keep silent. Things like that, someone breaks, and usually sooner rather than later. We're just not designed to keep secrets."

"So some unknown person took the baby," Ellen said, and swore at a driver who tried to cut her off, edging her way into merging lanes toward the bridge. "Or it's dead. Already long long dead."

"Maybe. If so, then why would our guy disappear, too? If the

171

baby's gone, and momma's off the map…"

"Because whoever deaded them, deaded him too?" Ellen had never been a delicate flower, despite Sergei's occasional attempts to protect her from the grimmer aspects of life. "Fact: momma seems to have gone missing, no forwarding address. Fact: baby is missing. We have no idea if the baby is with momma or not but since she checked out beforehand without a diaper bag, probably not. When mommy and daddy and baby make all missing, they're either together, or mostly—all dead. Right?"

"You've been listening." Listening, and reading. Danny handled mostly missing person cases, and a lot of them, she'd discovered, didn't end with happily ever afters. "All right, let's assume that there is a connection, because the coincidence required for them to *not* be is too large to start with."

They passed back into Manhattan, and she glanced at him, waiting for instructions on where to go, even as she was cutting off a cabbie who tried to cut her off. Danny winced, and she grinned. There wasn't much she felt a hundred percent confident on, but the ability to drive in city traffic was one of them. If all else failed, she'd go to work as a cabbie.

"First, we disprove what's disprovable. Go visit Rashada in the morgue, see if anything came his way in the past eight months. I'll man the phones, see if baby-girl Doe was dropped into any foster homes or orphanages."

"You think that might've happened? I mean, wouldn't someone notice, or…"

"Yeah, it's doubtful. But sometimes human cluelessness trumps out. And the child *might* be entirely human, on the outside…" He sighed. "At least until she hits puberty. It would be better if we found her before then."

"If she's alive."

"Yeah. If she's alive."

Ellen focused on driving, then. She'd saved someone last night. Was it too much to hope that they could save this one, too? Maybe. She tried not to think about it, as though that might distract fate from one tiny baby.

Alfred was exhausted. His feet hurt, his eyes felt like they'd been washed in sand, and he could only imagine how frantic his wife must be, assuming that she hadn't finally gotten fed up and tossed all of his things onto the front lawn.

No. She wouldn't do that. She'd put up with so much, she'd put up with this, but she'd be worried. He should call her, he should have taken the chance when he was in the police station to call her, but back then it had seemed like a bad idea. Now, twenty-four hours later, all he could think about was her sleeping alone in their bed, her hand stretched out to where he should be, and finding only a cold mattress.

His companion settled him down on the sidewalk, and inclined its head toward the house on front of them.

"What makes you think the baby's here, more than any of the other places? How can you even know it's anywhere near here? That this isn't a wild goose chase?"

"I know. Go. Talk to them." Again, it was saying.

Alfred had been given no choice in any of this. There had been a mysterious note on his desk one morning, reminding him of a one-time affair that he'd almost forgotten about, with a woman young enough to be his daughter, with the smoothest skin he'd ever touched, and eyes so pale brown they seemed nearly yellow.

"Your child is lost." the note had said, the handwriting spiky but readable. "You owe a life." Nothing more: no name, no return address, nowhere to start even looking. So he'd done the only thing he could, he'd hired a professional, told him the little he knew, and waited.

That hadn't been good enough, apparently, and the next thing he knew he'd been knocked off his feet—literally—by this creature, who insisted that the child be found *now*.

"I'm going to get arrested again," he muttered, trying to smooth down his hair and checked to make sure his jeans weren't any more stained that before. "And this time they're not going to let me go with a warning."

"I sniff. You ask."

Alfred cast an uncertain look at his companion, not sure how well that beaked nose could smell anything, but since it could easily tear him apart if he pissed it off, he did what he'd been doing: obeying orders.

A young woman answered the door, giving him a puzzled but friendly look. By now, he didn't really believe the infant was here—especially since the woman looked barely old enough to have sex, much less be caring for a baby—and when she shook her head and said they had no infant, he thanked her for her time, and left.

"They're moving her," his companion said. "One step ahead, all the time." It clacked its beak in frustration, and drummed its talons on the side of a postal box, making a heavy, metallic thrumming echo.

"Why is she so important?" Alfred asked, for what seems like the hundredth time. "If she's with good parents, why not leave her there?" All the houses they've checked have been nice, with people who seem decent enough." He had wanted to find her, out of responsibility—he wasn't a total shit—but a pair of young parents, people who *wanted* her, that was better than anything he could give her. And why the hell was this creature so determined to find her? It wasn't from any nasty impulse; the creature seemed legitimately worried.

"The child needs to be found," his companion said, likewise for the hundredth time. "They will not tell me. They will tell you."

No matter how long it took, hung unspoken in the air between them.

8

I was trying to get the new coffee maker, which I'd already dubbed Podzilla, running, when the office door creaked open cautiously, as though the person on the other side had been surprised by the door being unlocked, and wasn't sure who was on the other side.

"Boss. Did you sleep here?"

I hit Podzilla's start button, listening to its hiss of steam with a possibly erotic shiver of anticipation, and ignored the question as being beneath notice.

"Boss."

She'd been taking lessons in that voice from someone else. Either that, or she was developing a strong streak of Mom, too.

"No, I didn't," I reassured her. But I hadn't slept well, either. I finally gave up around four in the morning, and spent the rest of the night wandering the streets. It was weirdly soothing; half my genetics might crave green hills and free-running water, but everything else was a child of concrete and steel in general, and New York City in particular. There was an energy to the pre-dawn

176

hours that had nothing whatsoever to do with magic and everything to do with magic, if that made any sense at all. Even the darkest streets still felt the quiver of neon in the air, solitary traffic speeding and slowing to the lights, echoes of late-closing bars and early morning hustle, punctuated by trucks rattling in for pre-dawn deliveries and running through it all the constant awareness of life. New York wasn't the city that never slept so much as it was the city of overlapping shifts, where one person's bedtime was another person's wake-up call.

I'd given up and headed toward the office as the clouds were starting to lighten to pink. Ellen was here early, too, but a quick glance confirmed that she was neither bright-eyed nor bushy-tailed. She didn't drink coffee: I wasn't sure how she was still standing. I said as much.

"I'm young and resilient," she said. "But you will forgive me because I brought breakfast." She held up a bag, but my nose had already told me.

"Give. And talk." I fished out a brioche and put it on the counter next to the coffee maker, then put the bag down and waited.

"So yeah," and I could hear her taking off her coat and dropping it on the wooden coatrack, then sitting at her desk, the chair squealing slightly as she swiveled around. "I went to see Rashada, like you said. And then spent the next five hours going through her files, which are not, just so you know, digital. I have paper cuts on my paper cuts. But I can tell you that no newborn died that week coming from that hospital, and no non-human infant was brought into the morgue in the past nine months." She paused. " Rashada said she'd know if the baby wasn't human. Even half. Yes?"

"Maybe." The coffee machine let me know it was ready, and I pulled a double shot into my cup, and slammed it back. "Lilin can pass for human unless you're looking close." Like me. "I don't know what their insides look like, and never wanted to ask. But yeah—they're not human, so there'll be some differences that would ping for someone like Rashada." She'd cut into every fatae db in the past five years, no matter when they hit the slab. The local Talent Council had made sure of that. They wanted to know what was happening when, why and to whom. The fatae mostly weren't thrilled with the Council's nose poking into our business, but we'd learned the hard way we couldn't prevent it. Not entirely.

"That doesn't mean the baby's alive, through," Ellen said. "Whoever took her, they might have just dumped her."

I turned fast at that, a hot comeback on my tongue until I saw how miserable she looked at even mentioning it, and how she flinched a little, when I moved. Easy, boy. This is Shadow, you can still spook her way too easy. And what she'd said was true. Ugly, but true.

"If so, we may never know. But until we can prove all other leads are kaput, we don't assume that."

He was angry with her. Ellen knew she was too sensitive, too quick to assume she'd done something wrong, too fast to apologize. You spend ten years with everyone thinking you were crazy, a burden, a problem, you learned all of that. But she knew anger when she saw it, even when he was trying to bite it back, not take it out on her. She forced her breathing to stay even, soothing the static-jangled core inside her so she didn't destroy the brand-new coffee maker, or worse, his laptop in the back office.

"Don't assume anything." He was still lecturing her, his body tense like he was trying really hard not to yell, or throw something. Not that he would—not at her, anyway—but it still triggered every protective reflex she had, to make herself small, invisible, inoffensive. She placed her hands palm-down on the desk, taking

178

comfort in the heavy wooden weight of it. It wasn't the same as grounding, where she'd tie herself into the energy of the granite underfoot, letting it hold any sudden sparks or snaps in her current, but it was enough for now. She *knew* she wasn't in any danger, she just had to convince her body of that.

"You know I won't," she said mildly, and he sighed, all of a sudden the air going out of him. He ran his hands through his hair, the small, curved horns appearing briefly, then hidden again. She still had never seen him shoeless, so she didn't know if his feet were hoofed or not. She couldn't imagine his usual cowboy boots would be comfortable if they were, but…

"Yeah, I know," he was saying, and she forced her attention back into focus. "Sorry. This case…"

"Is it because," and she lifted one hand cautiously, making a vague gesture with it, "because, you know…"

"Because the baby's a cross-breed like me? No. And usually I'm better with infant abductions, there's less chance of something going wrong." He must have seen some expression change on her face, because he elaborated. "Teenagers, they're at risk. Young kids, seriously at risk. There are a lot of fucked up bastards out there who consider them easy or preferred prey. But babies… most times, they're stolen for the breeder biz. Adoptions for profit. So they're well taken care of, relatively speaking, and mostly given into good hands. I still want to get them back, but there's less…"

Ellen had seen enough to know what he wasn't saying. Less risk of abuse. The kind of stuff you couldn't ever rescue someone from, not really. She didn't feel capable of pushing any further; something else was bothering him but he'd have to figure it out on his own.

He flipped back to business. "So the mother's gone missing, and soon after the baby goes missing, and we've got no leads on either one of them. If the Lilin find anything, they'll tell us—if only to

179

keep us from poking into their business any further. So we go back to focusing on daddy, for the moment. Specifically, how he got the hell off that roof."

"Something winged took him." It was the only reasonable explanation, for Cosa levels of reasonable. "Unless we have a helicopter that's so silent that the woman inside the house doesn't hear it hovering over her head?"

"What, like a hang glider?" He shook his head, even as Ellen tried to figure out how a hang glider could swoop a full-grown man off his roof. "All right, so what? Not a great wyrm, they'd be too noticeable, even in the 'burbs. What else was large enough? And wouldn't be noticed?"

"How do you not notice something winged flying through your back yard?" But Ellen knew the answer to that already. The same way her family had not-seen any—all—of the things she had seen, over the years. Because they didn't *want* to see. All the things that had happened to her, around her, they had just not seen, so they wouldn't have to deal with it. You had to see before you could -

"Underneath."

Danny tilted his head to the side. "What?"

"Check underneath. That's what the raven said."

Narrowed eyes joined the tilted head. "A raven talked to you? Shadow, you need to *tell* me these things. Seriously—maybe Talent don't think about it, but every fatae knows: when a raven speaks to you: pay attention."

Ellen bit the inside of her cheek, to keep from responding. He was right, she hadn't known, hadn't thought about it that way. She'd been thinking of the bird as a bird, not... well, any of the things it *might* be. She had also thought that it was about her vision. But what if it wasn't?

"Underneath what?" she wondered, turning it around in her head.

"The roof," they both said at the same time.

Ellen hadn't returned the rental car the night before, extending their reservation through the end of the week. I wasn't sure if she was developing a twitch of precog, or just playing a hunch. The difference between the two was millimeters in my experience, anyway. If she was able to find consistent free street parking, we might have a new revenue stream in the making, through. Hire-a-parker could be seriously popular, especially around the holidays, and-

"We're here, boss."

The house wasn't anything particularly special: a well-maintained Colonial on a street filled with an assortment of similarly well-maintained houses, all built around the same time, probably mid-fifties. There weren't any white picket fences visible, but you could practically feel their ghosts running along the lines of every lawn.

"And why didn't we come here first?" I asked. Ellen glanced over at me as she scouted for a place to park, then decided this must be a Teaching Moment, because she just shrugged. "Because you hate coming out to Westchester?"

"I don't hate Westchester. I just find it pointless. No, we didn't come out here because by the time the client contacted us, she would have had time to set up anything she wanted us to see, and anything actually relevant would have been tidied up and put away, intentionally or not."

Ellen tapped the wheel with her fingers, frowning. "Is that pragmatism, or bitter cynicism?"

"A little of both, neither unwarranted. They're Council members, so she had the right to go to them for help, and instead went first to an outsider, and then to me. What does that tell you?"

181

"That our client wants us to find her husband, but she doesn't want a fuss. She knows the baby's half-fatae?"

"Or, more likely, she knows that the girl was young, and Lilin. Having a husband who cats around is one thing. Having one who gets off with a succubus… that's just tacky. I did do an Internet search on the neighborhood, though. God bless the Internet."

Ellen made a face, and I laughed. Yeah, all right, I wasn't above rubbing it in a little, occasionally. On the other hand, I couldn't move from one place to another by thinking about it, or any of the other things I'd seen her use current to do, so I figured we were about even.

She parked around the corner, and we walked back to the McConnell house. There was no car in the driveway, and a quick look inside the garage revealed empty space. Good. I hadn't planned on ringing the doorbell, but this made things easier. There was a ladder leaning against the side of the house, and I walked over to it, testing its sturdiness with a rough shake.

"Seems safe enough." Even to me, my voice didn't sound convinced.

"If a sixty-something guy could climb it, you can too," Ellen said. I didn't point out to her that I wasn't much younger; I had enough vanity to maintain the illusion that I was still in my late thirties, thank you very much. But I set my foot on the first rung, and started climbing. It was a little nerve-rattling, but I made it to the top and hauled myself onto the roof, looking over the side to see if Ellen was going to follow me.

"Nice view."

I didn't quite fall over the edge, but it was close. I turned and glared at Ellen, who was standing next to me. "Cough next time you Translocate, okay?" The line of sight from ground to roof must have been clear enough that she'd felt she could manage it without a spotter. "All right, we're up here. Now where do we actually *look?*" Trust a raven not to be specific, and there were a lot of tiles.

"Where had he been standing?"

"Over there," I said, pointing to the area near the chimney. "According to the police report, he'd been looking at the flashing around the chimney, to see if they needed to have someone come out before winter started."

We did a crab-crawl over there, neither of us trusting our balance enough to walk upright on the slightly-slanted roof. If any neighbors happened to look out their curtained windows to see us, they weren't inclined to come out and raise a fuss. God bless suburbia.

The tiles around the chimney looked intact, but we started lifting the edges with out fingernails, anyway, searching for something, anything that might explain the raven's words.

"You know the raven might–"

"Keep looking," I said. "Ravens elsewhere might be anything. A raven in a graveyard—in *that* graveyard, at *that* hour of the morning? Even if it was screwing with us, which is always a possibility, we can't ignore it."

It took us about fifteen minutes, and several splinters under fingernails, before Ellen let out a surprised, somewhat worried "oh."

"What?" I turned carefully, letting the shingle I'd been testing go back into position, and looked over at her. She held up her hand, and I heard myself go "oh," too.

She was holding a feather in her hand, the quill's point between forefinger and thumb. There wasn't any breeze, but it moved gently, the cloud-muted sunlight catching it just enough to illuminate the silvery tone of the vane.

"Fuck," I said. "Oh, fuck."

"What is it?" Ellen's voice was still worried, but I could tell she was fascinated by the feather, too. It was small, maybe six inches long, max, and could, if you weren't thinking about it, be mistaken for, well something ordinary, fallen from a dove's wing, maybe. But that particular shade of silver, the deep red of the shaft, clearly visible? That came from only one place.

"That's a gryphon feather," I told her, my mouth dry, but going for my best teacher-tone, rather than the flipped-out awe I was feeling. "The only fatae with silver feathers are gryphons. They're generally solitary, more than a little cranky, and pretty damned rare."

"So why was one so interested in our missing human? I mean, other than the missing child, there's nothing particularly unique or odd about Alfred. Why would a gryphon be interested in a cross-breed child that wasn't one of theirs?"

"I don't know." But even if Ellen didn't have any precog, my spidey senses were tingling.

9

They'd ended up at the edge of a park, after the last house was another no-go, the owner there an older woman who seemed to have no idea at all what Alfred was talking about. The fatae claimed it was following a trail, but Alfred wasn't sure he believed that any more. The child had been in all of these places? How long ago, and for how long, and why did they keep moving her? None of this made sense.

It was late afternoon, the park was deserted except for a couple at the far end, snuggling on a bench. He wanted, suddenly, to sit down, even on a cold bench, and just not move. He was beyond tired; he was weary. His core, never all that strong to begin with, was near-depleted, and the thought of reaching out to restock made his bones turn to ash. There was only so far a human could push himself, and he was nearly there.

The creature reached for him, clearly intending to hoist him into the sky and off to another house and another dead end. Alfred stepped back. "No. No more. Not again." He'd reached the end of his rope. "I can't do this anymore. It's insane, we're not getting anywhere, and I don't think you're right about where the infant is, anyway, because there's no way they can be shifting her like this, even with the best translocation skills ever. So no, no more."

"You must. You owe a life."

"I don't owe jack-shit. I don't even know for certain this child's mine, only just what you've told me. What happened to Kerrieon? Where is she? Why did she abandon the child like that? Why didn't she call me?"

"I didn't know."

That was the first actual answer he'd gotten from the creature. The problem was, that wasn't actually an answer at all.

"What the hell do you mean, you don't know? You knew to find me, so you must know something." He'd been on this insane hunt for three days, which was two days longer than he'd thought it would take, when the fatae landed on the roof and told him he was needed. Three days without decent sleep, without a bath, without a decent cup of coffee. He wasn't thinking straight any more, and he wanted it done.

"The child must be found."

"You keep saying that but you won't tell me why. Fuck that. Take me home." He was pissed, but not so pissed off that he forgot he was, effectively, stranded here in this town, and calling his wife to pick him up.

Screw it. He could deal with her yelling at him all the way home, so long as he got home. Turning on his heel with near-military precision, he walked away. Or tried to, anyway. The fatae's claws had been nearly gentle as they held him in flight, keeping him safe so far above ground, but now those talons dug into his flesh, the jacket and shirt no barrier.

"You owe a life."

Alfred stared across the park, seeing freedom out of reach.

"What the hell is your problem? You haven't shown me any proof that she's in danger! That was the only reason I came with you, the only reason I went looking, because I thought she was in danger. But so far—nothing. If she's in one of these houses, which I doubt, they're well-off enough to give her a proper life. But if you don't know *where* she is, how do you know she needs me?"

He couldn't shake off that claw, so he turned into it, uncomfortably close to that fierce beak, and the deep golden eyes glaring over it. "Unless you can tell me, right here and now, that you know for a fact that she needs my help, that she's in danger, and not being perfectly well cared for by whoever took her home from the hospital, then this. Is. Over."

"The child is not in danger. The child *is* danger." Those golden eyes were too wide, the pupils too small and black. Alfred felt he was in danger of falling forward, falling into them and never getting out.

"What?"

"The child. It is an abomination. It must not be allowed. Only humans thought it could be saved, should be saved. It should have never happened, should have been allowed to die."

"What?" Alfred knew he sounded like an idiot. He felt like one, too. "You're insane. Never mind about taking me home. I'll call Christie and deal with the fallout the way I should have two days ago."

Just saying it made him feel better, a little stronger. Yeah. He should have told Christie at the start. She was a clear thinker, she might have figured out a way to find the baby—or understood that it wasn't their matter to meddle in at all, that the baby was already with good parents and this crazy fatae was only trying to stir up trouble. He'd go home and tell her everything, and he could finish fixing the roof before winter hit.

"No."

"Yes." He stared at the fatae, his own eyes narrowed. "Enough. Whatever you think needs to be done, whatever you're planning to do, I'm out." If the creature needed him to find the baby, walking away was the best thing he could do, for both of them. Even if the kid wasn't his.

There was no warning, only the clack of the thing's beak, before a talon hit him across the face. Then again, the blow of one feathered arm against the chest, and another blow to the side of his head. None of them were made with any sort of precision, but the sheer force behind them made that less important, and Alfred went to his knees, his head ringing and his vision already starting to haze over.

He hoped the kid was his. He'd like to think his last act had been protecting his own.

10

Ellen was sitting on her desk, legs crossed under her, the gryphon feather in her hands. Or rather, hovering just above her hands, the quill's tip balanced pointing down onto her palm but not actually resting on the flesh. Little sparks of current flickered around it, which made me think that there was a hell of a lot more current actually in use, if I was able to see that much.

Fatae couldn't use magic, any more than a Null human could. But it ran in our bodies, according to all the reading I'd done, making us more attuned to it than non-Talent humans. I always—almost always—knew when it was being used around me, and it would take a skilled Talent to use it against me.

Damnable thing was, I seemed to know a lot of skilled Talent. Even when I was back on the force, it seemed like half the guys I knew on the street were high res. Just lucky, I guess.

"Anything?"

She shook her head, letting the feather come to rest. "No. I mean, there's a sense of it there, the guy himself, and definitely a guy, but... I don't know if its because I'm not strong enough, or because I don't know enough about gryphons. When Genevieve taught me this, we used a strand of PB's fur, and a drop of Sergei's blood, and I was able to identify them right away, but…"

"But you know them both. All right, get yourself settled down, and come back into the office."

Any current-use she did, she did out here. It would be easier to replace another coffee maker and a mini-fridge than it would my laptop, safe-lined drawer or no. But it would take her a little while to shake down her current and smooth it out, or whatever it was they did. I went into the inner office and closed the door behind me, taking a moment.

Ellen had been right: this case was shaking me a little. It wasn't the baby-in-jeopardy part; I knew my weaknesses and was used to dealing with them. Kids in jeopardy hit all my buttons, yeah. But it wasn't that, and it wasn't that this was a cross-breed, either. I didn't think that was it, anyway.

I sat down at my desk and pulled the laptop out of its drawer, booting it up at the same time and checking email. The formal reports from Rashada, confirming what she'd told Ellen. A note from Fagan at the precinct, confirming that no known female fatae bodies had shown up anywhere without clear I.D. Now that I knew what breed she'd been I could guarantee that she would be a Jane Doe: Lilin who ended up in bad places generally didn't have soft landings.

"Boss?" Ellen came in just as my cell phone rang. I held up a hand for her to stay where she was, just in case. Static was a natural by-product of Talent.

"Hendrickson. Yeah, I got it." I waited. "Really? All right." I didn't insult Fagan by asking if she was sure: she wouldn't have called me if he wasn't. "Yeah, I should be able to confirm. Can you send—all right, thanks. Yeah, take care."

I hung up the phone and gestured for Ellen to come all the way in even as I was checking to see if the promised email had come in.

"They found our missing man. He's at Mother of Mercy."

"Hospital, not morgue. He's alive?"

"Only just. No ID, but they're pretty sure it's our guy."

"So what happened to him?"

"That's the question, isn't it? I've got a file coming in...now." I paid extra for high-speed internet. I would have been better off spending the money on beer and pissing it away. But eventually the file downloaded.

I clicked on the attachments, and grunted.

"What?" Ellen came all the way into the office, leaning over my shoulder to see better. I could feel the gentle static hum of her core for a moment, like standing next to a portable generator, then it was locked down, still and cool.

I touched my hand to the screen, tapping one area of the photograph. "Those look like claw marks?"

"Yeah," she agreed. "There, and...there." She didn't touch the screen, but I saw what she was looking at. "The bruising—he was beaten?"

"By someone, or something with a very heavy hand." Or wings. "McConnell's in no position to answer questions; they're not sure he's going to remember anything when he wakes up, assuming he does wake up. We need to find that gryphon."

There was a heavy weight of silence over my shoulder, and I could tell she was thinking. Technically, the case was over. We'd been hired to find the missing man, and we'd done that, more or less. But there were questions that needed to be answered—a missing child to be found—and nobody else was going to do it, if I didn't. If *we* didn't.

"Boss, you're awesome at finding people, solving puzzles, that overt, detail-oriented stuff. Given time, you could learn where a gryphon hangs out. But getting it? I mean, laying hands on it? If you need something retrieved..."

191

"As a Retriever. I know." I shut the lid of the laptop, and stared at the matte black surface. "You're injuring my professional pride, Shadow." She wasn't wrong, though. I could find the gryphon, but it would take time, and odds were I'd never get anywhere near it. But Wren... the Wren could.

"Call your mentor. Let's see how well she plays with others."

I'd barely had time to put the order in for two large pizzas—Talent ate like horses when they were using a lot of current—before I heard voices in the outer office. Wren must have Translocated, which meant no Sergei. I was outnumbered.

"Hi." I stood in the doorway and looked at the two women standing there. If you didn't know, you'd think Ellen was the more impressive one, tall and broad-shouldered, with glossy dark skin and hair, while the woman next to her was slighter, mousy-brown and seemingly insignificant. The emphasis would be on "seemingly." Retrievers, by their very nature, deferred the eye and muddled memories. Had Wren chosen to become an assassin.... Fortunately, she was at heart a kleptomaniac, not a killer.

"I hear you've got a job that needs my delicate touch."

"We getting the mentor discount?" Sergei wasn't just her partner, he was her business manager, too. He'd have a suitably pithy comment about her working for free.

"I'll call in a favor at a later date," she said, and I nodded, agreeing. As much as I hadn't wanted to call her in, she'd be at death's door before she asked me for help, and at that point I'd have given it anyway. We were just saving face, here.

"I have a feather from the gryphon's wing, I think." Ellen said. "I already used it to try to trace him, but I wasn't able to get anything."

"Underwing," I said. "From the size, probably close to the claws."

"Nothing else?"

"Photos of his victim. The guy's in the hospital now; if you needed to be in contact with him…"

"Huh." She considered that. "No. Let's try without, first. I'd be able to slip in unseen but it would take some time, and it might not be needed." She held out her hand, and Ellen placed the feather down on her palm.

"Yo, wait." I went back into my office and shut the laptop down completely and put it in the shielded drawer, and then turned off my cell phone and put it in the drawer as well. I'd heard stories about what happened to electronics around Wren, and my replacement budget was already stretched to its limit. Then I unlocked the drawer below it, and took out my service pistol, and loaded it.

"All right. Do you need anything?"

"For you to shut up and stay out of the way?" Wren's voice was low, sweet, and utterly focused on the feather in her hand.

"I can do that."

This was the first time I'd seen Ellen interact with her mentor. My Shadow wasn't a Retriever, that wasn't her skillset. But she was a Seer, and I was guessing that they were going to use that to tie into Wren's own skills. Magic—current—was beyond my pay grade. I leaned against the wall and, as per orders, shut up and stayed out of the way.

"I have the feather. I'll be able to work a seeking cantrip, I think. It's the same thing I use when I'm scoping out a site, doing a little advance research. You've seen me do it."

Ellen nodded, intent on her mentor's words. "I should follow along?"

"No. I want you to go into your core and open up. See what I stir up."

She said "see" but even I knew she meant See.

"All the way open," Wren said, glancing up from the feather to look at Ellen directly. "I'm here, and this place is as grounded as anywhere in the city. It's an old building, solid foundations, built on bedrock. You can ground all the way down, brace yourself that way. And goat-boy over there will watch over us physically, right?"

I hefted the pistol in my hand. "Anything that comes in, deals with me, first."

"Try not to shoot us while you're doing it."

"If I yell duck, don't quack."

Pre-fight nerves, even though there wasn't a fight brewing. Ellen was looking back and forth between us, then down again at the feather, and I wanted to do something say something to bolster her courage. I didn't. This wasn't my place; Wren was her mentor. I was just her boss.

"Breathe, ground and center." Wren's voice was soft, steady, and Ellen exhaled and then drew a fresh breath, her shoulders softening, her hands resting against her thighs.

The feather rose off Wren's palm, hovering in the air between them, dancing slightly as though tugged by a thread. The air was thick and electric, and I could practically hear the new coffee maker shorting out. I hoped Ellen had thought to unplug it, but I wasn't going to interrupt to check.

"Feather, fly
Return to the bone
But remain"

I hadn't expected spellcasting to be quite so...poetic. The sense of static in the air increased, and the feather spun around frantically, turning quill-side up and then pointing back down again.

"Let me See." Ellen's incantation or whatever they called it, was simple, but heartfelt. She reached up a hand and closed her fingers around the feather, stopping its movement. Her entire hand, underneath the skin, was alive with a pulsing yellow-green neon, like… like nothing. I felt a little ill, watching, so I looked away. Wren's hands were blue-green. The feather was sparkling with a paler silver glitter, turning faster and faster within Ellen's grasp.

"He's dying. He's hurt so bad inside, and he was so tired, he's dying."

My first impulse was to grab my notebook and write down her words, but that would have required putting down the gun. I listened as hard as I could, trying to remember.

"Feather, fly," Wren repeated. "Return to the bone, to the bone."

The feather quivered again, and Ellen cried out as though the quills had suddenly got hot, but she didn't let go. I kept my grip loose on the grip of my handgun, and breathed out, trying for my own form of grounding, the way we'd been taught to do before a raid or during a standoff.

"In a building, an old building. It's built a nest but I can't see where it is, can't…oh."

This was the first time I'd seen her try for a Seeing, rather than having one come on her, and as far as I knew, the first time she'd consciously tried to scry for someone we knew was still alive. The only difference I could see was the play of current-light under her skin; that was new. She was facing away from me so I couldn't tell if the glazed look in her eyes was the same. The shiver in my horns and the back of my neck was less for what was happening in front of me than the potential even I could feel, working beneath the surface.

When I'd first met Ellen, I knew that others were wary of her. I'd understood why, intellectually—but now I *knew* why, bone-deep. A Storm Seer wasn't just a high-res Talent. Ellen was a perfect conduit, a lightning rod that could *use* the lightning that hit her. If she was trained.

195

That was why Wren was her mentor. And some day, maybe, the student would be more powerful than the teacher.

I was, weirdly, calm about that. I knew Ellen. She was a good kid. Careful, cautious, and maybe a little too cautious, yeah, after the family life she'd had, but that was no bad thing, either. Power corrupts, but only so far as we let it.

"I have the nest," Wren said, her voice thin but steady. I'd known her for years, but never seen her when she was working. I realized I was holding my breath. "An abandoned building, yes. Not a warehouse; maybe an old school? Further west… Trenton, maybe, one of the older, smaller cities. Smart, to stay the hell out of Madame's territory."

Gryphons were fierce, but you didn't fuck with a centuries-old Great Wyrm who claimed Manhattan for her own, no.

"I think I've got him," the Retriever said, finally. "Nice lead, Ellen. We can—"

"There's something else," Ellen said. Her face had lifted toward the ceiling, and I half-expected a bolt of current-lightning to come through the roof and hit the tip of her nose. Maybe it did; this Null couldn't see it. "There's a connection." She held the feather again, this time so tightly the edges were crushed. "The man and the gryphon…blood."

"Spilled blood, from the fight?"

Wren glared at me, like I should shut up. I glared back.

"No." Ellen shook her head, and her hand shook, too. "Contained. Shaped, formed…."

Wren lifted her hand as though to touch Ellen's hand and the feather, but stopped. Yeah, I didn't think that would be a good idea right now, either.

"New form. New life. Three swirls of blood, swirling together."

Wren looked confused. I, on the other hand, knew exactly what my Shadow was saying. The baby wasn't a cross-breed, she was a tri-breed. Alfred's daughter… the gryphon's grand-daughter.

"Fuck me," I said, half-awed, half-horrified. "That's not good."

11

Wren frowned at me, a truly terrifying sight. "Is that even possible?"

"Possible, sure. Probable? Likely? Good? No and no and no."

"Why?" Ellen asked. "I mean, why's it a bad thing?"

"People—and by people I mean fatae, specifically—flip out over cross-breeds. It's like, oh god, like miscegenation in the 1930's. Cats and dogs, living together, end of the world etc etc. Except for a tri-breed… that could actually happen. End of the world, I mean. Not in the Mayan prophesy way, but people flipping like mammals and doing incredibly stupid shit in reaction."

I didn't have a high opinion of most fatae, when it came to hard-wired speciesist reactions. I didn't have a high opinion of humans, either. Even a year on the force of any major city will burn optimism out of you.

"So why–"

"We need to find the gryphon, if we're going to get any answers. Wren, can you Translocate me there?"

Her eyes narrowed, then she shook her head. "Third-party

transloc isn't my thing. I've done it, but it's…iffy. And Ellen isn't skilled enough yet to risk that distance, to a place she's never been."

"Fuck." I could feel the timetable running out on us. Yeah, the guy we'd been hired to find had been found, no thanks to us. But there was still a baby out there, and none of us believed that the gryphon had its best interest at heart, not after the beat-down it had presumably given daddy.

"What about Pietr? I mean, since you felt comfortable enough to call him in for other stuff."

Wren looked at me. I looked at the ceiling. Ellen didn't sound pissed, but that didn't mean she wasn't. I needed to remember to tell her when I did things like that going forward, clearly. "Yeah. Ask him."

There was a moment of blankness in her eyes, and a couple of minutes later, the soft sucking-pop noise of someone Translocating in.

"I don't suppose there's any way to lock you people out?"

Pietr, being a PUP, took the question seriously. "There is. I'll teach hot-stuff here when we get back. Where are we going?"

"Not we. Me."

"What?" Ellen started to protest.

"Just me." I stared Ellen down, which only took a minute. Valere, wisely, kept her mouth shut. I considered tucking the pistol into my waistband, then decided keeping it in my hand was the less-stupid move. "This is my gig, Shadow. You're not trained"— not ready—"for it. Yet."

The "yet" placated her. For now.

I hate being Translocated. It's roughly akin to being blindfolded, thrown into one of those sideways carnival rides, and then dumped out somewhere other than where you started, with no idea of what's waiting for you on the other end. No, actually, that's *exactly* what it's like. Also, it makes me want to throw up, which isn't the best way to come into an unknown situation.

Especially when the unknown situation contains a pissed-off, bloody-taloned gryphon.

I landed square on my feet, but facing a bare, brick wall. Behind me, I heard the rustle-whisper of feathers against feathers, and made sure the gun was secure in my hand, barrel pointing down, before I turned.

"It's more polite to call ahead, rather than drop in unannounced." The voice was dry, with an undercurrent of clacking to the consonants.

"Your number was unlisted," I said, letting my wrist loosen. It didn't sound like our suspect was about to attack any time soon, but I wasn't letting down my guard entirely. The gryphon was about ten feet away, seated on a wide sofa, its long, tawny tail curled around its hindquarters, the barbed tip twitching slightly. The wings were folded, shifting occasionally the way someone might tap their fingers, and the head was...

I hadn't been prepared for how gorgeous that falcon's head would be, great golden eyes and sharply curved beak not at all alien, or even unfriendly. But dangerous, absolutely dangerous.

"You can put the gun away, faun."

"If it's all the same to you, I'll keep it out," I said. Without my usual cap, my horns were probably obvious enough to give away my fatae blood, but it was entirely possible that he could sniff it, too. Which meant he knew I was human, also. Considering his behavior so far, I wasn't going to assume peaceful intentions, faced with that fact.

"Oh...that." The gryphon didn't really have facial expressions— it didn't have much of a face, period—but there might have been a hint of apology in his voice. "I lost my temper."

"Just a bit, yeah." I kept my breathing steady, and my gaze direct, but unchallenging. Every confrontation with a perp had this moment, where they had to decide how much trouble they were in, and how much more trouble you could bring down on them. "So now you're looking at, what? Kidnapping, assault... maybe first degree manslaughter..."

The gryphon didn't drop its gaze, but the feathers on the top of its head smoothed enough that I figured it wasn't going to attack, at least not just yet. "You can hand me over to the Council later," it said. "We need to find it."

"It?" I wasn't playing dumb, exactly, just waiting for the gryphon to come clean, and maybe tell me something new.

"The offspring. It should never have existed, and it must not fall under the wrong influences."

"The offspring, as you call it, is...what, your child, too? Grandchild?" Clearly it didn't have any paternal feelings going on.

He tilted that beaked head, and looked at me like I'd just said the dumbest thing in the history of dumb. "It should never have existed. Someone did this intentionally. Manipulated. Caused."

Great, a gryphon with paranoia and delusions of conspiracy. "Why?"

"Prophesy."

Oh for the love of—I took a step back, scanning the room for another chair. The only one I saw, I wouldn't trust to hold the weight of a coat, much less a person. "Founder Ben broke us of that, centuries ago. Nobody believes in prophesies any more."

"Perhaps they should." And by they, he clearly meant me.

"Right." I'd talked crazies out of their corner before, just not recently. I was out of practice. "Any particular prophesy in mind?"

He clacked his beak, and sighed. "Choose the poison you wish to ingest. The whisper, the threat, of many bloods in one flesh resurfaces with regularity. But the most recent was specific enough to reference a human child with wings on her back and original sin in her...heart."

I was betting heart wasn't the original placement. The jokes were too easy to make about the Lilin, which probably had as much to do with their reclusiveness as anything else. Some folk can't help hating what they want, especially once they discover it doesn't always want them back.

"So you think you were manipulated into sleeping with the ... the Lilin was your daughter, right? You didn't put the beat-down on your own son?" Nobody had suggested our missing man was anything other than human, but hey, people have been wrong about me, too.

"The girl was my offspring." He didn't seem happy about it. I couldn't tell if he was a bigot, or just embarrassed at having let his feathers down with a Lilin. "I did not know she was with child, or with what. Only after the fact was I informed."

And then he'd decided to get his grandbaby back himself. But why? Wait, he'd said influence, that the kid shouldn't fall under the wrong influences. So he was the right one? Or he thought daddy dearest would have been, before he beat the crap out of him? I hate dealing with crazies.

"So the folk who've taken her, their plan is...what? To raise the child as some end-of-times priestess? To sacrifice her? To..."

"To study her," he said, and damned if you couldn't sneer with a beak. "To see if there's a way to bring all the breeds into one."

"Well, it's nice to know we've tempered our magical fatalism with science," I said, wryly. Still, no matter how crazy they were— or weren't—if they intended to study her, or god help us, breed her, they were going to keep her alive and healthy, at least until puberty. That was one relief. But we needed to find her, and get her away from crazy people—and I was including grandpa in that category for now.

"So where is she?"

"If I knew that, do you think I would be wasting time with that idiot human?" An agitated gryphon's wingspread was impressive, and my hand may have tightened around the grip of my gun just a bit, even as I recognized the soft pop of an incoming Translocation. This loft was starting to get a bit crowded.

"I know." Ellen, her voice firm, like it was no big deal she'd just shown up in the middle of a gryphon's temper tantrum. "I know how to find her."

12

I spun around, and glared at Ellen, utterly forgetting—without actually forgetting—about the irate fatae behind me. "How the hell—"

"I know you well enough to follow," she said, answering the question I hadn't asked, and I filed that information away for later use. Right now I didn't want her hopping around to unknown spots but...yeah, that could be a definite plus, in sticky situations. And come with some potential problems, too. "We'll talk about your hop-skotching-into-danger later," I said out loud. "You said you can track the baby?"

"It's...not simple, exactly. But yeah, I think I can track her."

"With current?" The gryphon seemed torn between scorn and annoyance. Clearly, he didn't have much use for humans. Or Talent.

"With current," she said, echoing his tone. "Yeah."

I held up a hand, to get a word in edgewise. "What're the others up to?"

"They went home—but they're listening in case we need

backup." In other words, waiting for a ping. She gave the gryphon a glare. He glared right back, that tail lashing again, and for a moment I thought I was going to have to break up a hissing match.

"Children. Focus, please. So what's the deal with the kid?" I said to Ellen.

She gave the gryphon another glare, as though warning it to keep its claws off the two-legs, and turned to me. "It's simple, really. Most cantrips are, when you break them down, it's...." She looked at me, then the gryphon, and realized that neither of us gave a damn about the make-up or break-down of her spell, only if it would work or not.

"Okay. I um... I need a feather. Please?" She looked at the gryphon, and I could sense her trying not to flinch or squeak. I couldn't exactly blame her.

The gryphon—whose name we still hadn't got—studied her and then, with a single lash of its tail, reached up and plucked a long, silvery feather from its left shoulder. It didn't come out easily, and I winced, even if he didn't.

She took it carefully, almost reverently, and that seemed to settle him down a bit.

"I'm Danny, by the way," I said. "That's Ellen."

"Faosullvaant ."

I wasn't sure I could say that without a beak to clack, so I just inclined my head in acknowledgement of the information. "I'd say it was a pleasure to meet you, but not really. No offense."

"None taken."

"Both of you, hush." Ellen pulled something out of her jeans pocket, unstoppering it with her teeth and spitting the cork into the corner. She then dipped the quill into the vial. It came out stained a deep black.

Blood. She had blood in the vial.

"Do I want to know where that came from?"

"We needed the connection."

So, while I was chatting up Winged McLoon, Wren—I was presuming Wren—went into the hospital and took a blood sample from a comatose man. At least I didn't have to worry about anyone seeing her. And any worry about morality got left behind somewhere in my second year on the force. So I let it slide.

"You can do this, with that?"

"I'm a Seer. Seeing is what I do, right? This will help me focus on what I want to See."

"Right." Bonnie had explained to me once that Will was the most important thing when shaping current. Will, and Control. I didn't doubt Ellen's Will...

She held the feather up at eye level, dipped the point into the blood just enough to darken the tip, and turned it slowly, the way you would a key in a lock you weren't quite sure of, or if you were trying not to make any noise. The gryphon leaned forward, apparently interested despite himself. Well, it was his feather, after all.

"Generation to generation, blood to bone. Show me."

It didn't have the poetic nuance of Valere's cantrips, but from the sparking around her hand, I was betting it did the trick. Words were mostly showmanship, from what Bonnie'd said, more than a few times. You put on a show to convince yourself you knew what you were doing, and impress anyone who might likewise doubt.

The feather quivered and then—in a snap of sparks— disappeared.

"Where..."

Ellen's face had that look again. The one that said she was Seeing something.

"Wheels. A sea of wheels, and pavement, and shoes. People walking...standing. Glass and chrome."

I waited, but that was it, nothing specific enough to identify. But I had a hunch of my own.

"Look up," I directed her. "Lift your gaze."

Her chin tilted up, but her eyes were looking somewhere else. Hopefully, up.

"Streets, storefronts. Large glass windows, filled with things." Her head tilted to the side a little, and I was amused to recognize one of my own physical "don't bother me I'm thinking" quirks in her body. Well, I did call her Shadow... "A large sign, overhead. Green. Hanging down. A name? A... fruit?" Her face look puzzled for a moment, her own personality cracking through the Seer. We weren't going to get much more, if she didn't See it now.

Green sign...name... plate glass .... A fruit... I ran it through my own knowledge of the area, hoping against hope they hadn't gone out of the city, or into one of the remote pockets I hadn't wandered, or hadn't been too damaged or gentrified beyond recognition.

"A name of a fruit," she said, decisive now, and I laughed in relief.

"The Upper East Side. She's seeing the Upper East Side." J.G. Melon, home of one of the best burgers in New York City, and possessor of a large green sign hanging from the side of their building. "Huh, hide a stroller in a sea of strollers. Not isolated, buried. Not too shabby..."

"I have her," Ellen said. "I know where she is. But it's right *now*."

The gryphon got up from his bench, and I was suddenly aware of how thickly-muscled that body was. Not huge—maybe eight feet tall and five across the shoulders, but *solid*. "Then let us go," he said, extending one wing down, a clear invitation. I was— beyond dubious, but Ellen stepped forward without hesitation, and

207

considering the alternative was to haul out on mass transit—
which would take forever—or be held in those claws....

I got on.

One of the things I love and despair of about New York City—
and Boston and Chicago, for that matter—is how a fatae can walk
down the street and people look right at him and don't react.
Maybe a flicker of an eyelid and then it's "oh, well, okay then" and
they move on. In Los Angeles, people gawp. Down South, they do
a faint oh dear and turn away. Outside of the cities... it can get
ugly. But the big northern cities? Yeah, whatever pal, I get weirder
than you in my breakfast cereal.

Then again, if you saw a gryphon, twice as big as a linebacker
and three times as cranky, would *you* stare, much less get in his
way?

Ellen stopped on the corner, and lifted her chin, pointing not to
the restaurant, but the French cafe across the street. "She's in
there."

"Hide a stroller in a sea of strollers," I said, looking at the rows
of baby carriages that probably cost as much as a months' rent on
the office, parked outside the cafe. "Not isolated, buried. Smart.
Also pretty much impossible to find..."

"Without magic. Yes." The gryphon flicked one talon, unhappy
at being shown up by a Human, Talent or otherwise. "So now
what?"

"Now we steal a baby," Ellen said. "Let's see if I've learned
anything useful from Genevieve. You guys stay here and make a
distraction."

Before I had a chance to say anything, she had gone inside. I
knew what she was about to do, and she was right, it was the best
chance we had. But having someone in my employ use the same
tactics I was usually investigating... it made me nauseated.

Our best chance at a distraction would draw the Council's attention. But with luck, it would draw it away from the kid, not towards.

"Do something really obnoxiously impressive," I told Faosullvaant. "Ideally without actually hurting anyone."

The gryphon looked at me like I was an oversized and not-particularly-tasty rabbit, then turned away, his wings coming out and extending. I got out of the way—barely—as he turned. The wings were large, but they were as graceful as a ballerina's arms, and hit exactly what he intended them to.

I flinched as the fire hydrant's top burst open, a heavy stream of water rising a few feet into the air before turning into a fountain. Okay, that was impressive, but it wasn't going to get a lot of people anything more than wet and pissy -

And then he launched himself into the air, his lion's body in full leap into the air like a carousel carving, catching the full brunt of the water on the underside of his wings.

And what had been ordinary water, shaken off those silver feathers, became a kaleidoscope of rainbows shimmering from his shoulders to his tail, magic in motion, a thousand liquid hummingbirds before they splashed back down to the pavement. Everyone, and I mean every. Damn. One. On the block stopped, and stared.

And then he was gone.

"Did you see that?"

"That was awesome."

"Are they filming the new Marvel movie here?"

"Dude. I'm fucking soaked."

And then the moment was over, and everyone went back to whatever they'd been doing, shaking off the water or shaking their heads and messaging their friends, but walking away and not looking back. That was when I realized that Ellen had walked past me, something bundled in her arms. She kept moving, not looking back or around, her stride steady and sure as though she had every right to be carrying that baby in her arms.

I stepped into the street and hailed a cab.

Ellen walked away from the cafe, her heart pounding hard enough to break a rib, her ears ringing from alarms that hadn't gone off. The baby was surprisingly heavy, but easy enough to carry, almost as though she *wanted* to be taken away.

Ellen thought about trying to cast a cantrip to keep the baby quiet, or keep anyone from stopping her, but the main thing Genevieve said about retrieving—the few times her mentor would even talk about it—was that the best way to hide is to be exactly like everyone else in a crowd. So, no more current than she'd normally have running, and the stress and relief mixed in her expression could be any new mom, trying to get through her day, and her shoulder bag could pass for a diaper bag, if needed. Hopefully.

"Hush darling, we'll be home soon," she told the baby. The little face screwed up for a moment, as though about to cry, and then a tiny fist knocked against one soft, entirely human-looking cheek, and she soothed back into sleep.

Ellen exhaled, and headed for the next subway entrance. Head down, feet moving, and if getting her subway card out of her pocket was more effort, with a baby in her arms, nobody gave her a second look. She couldn't relax enough to recharge, though, and she could feel her muscles starting to shake with exhaustion. How did Genevieve *do* this?

Despite all of her fears, they made back to the office stop without anyone stopping her, or the baby starting to cry. In fact, the infant was so quiet she kept checking, nervously, that it was still breathing. She'd always heard that infants cried all the time, but this one seemed to prefer sleeping.

Surprisingly, the gryphon was waiting for her on the street. How he knew where to go, she didn't know, and she wasn't in the mood to ask, either. She glared at him, daring him to do something, make one move that she didn't like. Current moved in her core, alert to her mood.

The feathers on the top of his head, and the side of his neck fluttered slightly, but that might have been the breeze. Maybe. Where the hell was the boss?

13

Ellen wasn't happy with the fatae hanging around, but she acknowledged that he had as much right—maybe even more, being a relative—as she did. And if anyone came after her, or the baby, it would be some defense, anyway, even if just the "it's not kidnapping, look, here's grandpa" sort.

But Danny had better show up, *soon.*

The three of them made an odd grouping in the elevator; the gryphon barely fit, even with his wings furled tightly around his body. Once inside the office, the wings relaxed a little, and he took up the far corner of the front room, his golden eyes watching them carefully. Cautious, alert to anything that might happen.

"It's a baby," she said in disgust. "Just a baby, not even a toddler, which is when they get really scary." She'd babysat enough of them when she was a teenager to remember that. The gryphon just lurked, and watched, and didn't say anything.

"Yeah, all right. The coffee's on the counter behind you, if you want some. There's soda in the fridge. Just... Don't talk to me right now." Not that there seemed much chance of that.

She pulled her sweater off the back of the chair, and created a nest of sorts on the desk, weaving current into it so that it stayed in the right shape. If there was a small protection charm woven in as well, it wasn't as though anyone would be able to tell. The baby scrunched her face again, and let out a little sigh, and a tiny bubble of spit formed at the corner of her mouth. Ellen wasn't sure if that was adorable, or disgusting. "Hello, sweetie, aren't you a sweetie?" She unwrapped the blankets, wondering if maybe the boss had stopped to pick up diapers and formula, because otherwise someone was just going to have to turn around and go out again. "You look human... ten fingers, ten toes..."

The door opened behind her, the sound of Danny's cowboy boots a familiar noise against the linoleum. She risked a glance away from the baby, and saw that he was carrying a bag from the drug store down the street. Good.

He put the bag down on the floor with a soft-sounding thunk, and looked over her shoulder just as the baby opened her eyes.

"Huh. Well, there's that then," Danny said, an odd tone in his voice.

"Definitely not human," Ellen agreed. She lifted the now-awake baby in her arms, and turned, stepping away from Danny as she did so. "Your granddaughter," she said to Faosullvaant. "I don't suppose you know her name?"

The gryphon looked like he wanted to be anywhere but there, but Ellen didn't let him escape, stepping forward just enough that the baby caught sight of him. Chubby little arms flew out to the side, fingers working as though she was trying to grab at him.

The gryphon looked at her then, two pairs of golden eyes meeting for the first time. Something in him seemed to break, quietly. "Her grand-dam's name was Marciad."

"That'll work. Hello, Marciad"

213

"Still think she's an abomination?" Danny was leaning against the desk now, watching all three of them.

That beak clacked again, and Ellen though that maybe she was starting to "read" gryphon, because she knew it was thought, not irritation, that was behind it. "Yes. But it is not her fault that she exists. My daughter bears the blame for that, and she has gone beyond responsibility."

Dead then, or somewhere out of reach forever. Ellen wasn't sure which might be worse.

"She can never know what she is," the gryphon went on. "No-one should be able to use her, ever."

Danny nodded immediately, although she suspected he had his own reasons that had nothing to do with whatever grandpa was afraid of. "Agreed. Although if she starts to show—"

"A problem for another day?"

"Yeah, okay."

"Great, now that you've got her life all planned out for her, where's she going to go?" Ellen would have called them on their typical male BS, saying what Marciad could or couldn't be, but the chubby little hand trying to grab her nose now had all of her attention. "Don't do that, baby-girl. Stop. Help?"

Danny removed the fingers from Ellen's nose, and lifted the child away from her. "Hello, sweetness," he cooed at her, and she went right for his horns. He laughed, like they were ticklish, but didn't remove her hands. "You're going to be a handful and a half, aren't you darling?"

"What are we going to do with her? I mean, I don't think grandpa there wants her, and her parents…"

"Mom's gone, and dad's not really set up to handle this, no." Danny coaxed the baby into settling down, letting her grab at his own fingers. "Her mother's people said they'd take her. They're pretty mellow, as breeds go, and she'll be safe there." Isolated, he meant, and she heard, even unspoken. "And they always have kids running around, so one more won't raise eyebrows. If our gryphon buddy says she won't manifest feathers or a beak, I'm willing to take that on trust, but other breeds mingle a little less obviously, and those eyes are always going to be a question mark. Besides, she may not seem very Lilin-like right now, but better she be there when she hits puberty, just in case."

He went into the inner office, baby still in his arms, and she heard him sit down, and pick up the phone. Presumably to call the Lilin House. Or maybe to order pizza…it was Friday, right? She checked the calendar: yeah it was Friday.

They'd managed a happy ending, despite the odds. Their missing man was home, and Lilin House would take the baby in: they'd said so, knowing what the baby was, and Danny thought they were telling the truth. Whyever she'd been born, whatever her mother might have thought would happen, whatever she grew up to be, they would take her in, protect her. They'd make sure that Marciad doesn't spend her life being looked at oddly, as a freak, forever out-of-place. Danny would call that a win.

Ellen walked past the gryphon and reached down to pull a soda out of the fridge, taking it back to her desk and sitting down to sort through the mail. She slit open the first envelope, smiling. Boss might call it a win, but she called it a promise, kept.

An Afterward, and an Appreciation

In 2002, I had the first glimmer in my mind of the world that would become the Cosa Nostradamus, a world where some humans could channel the magic known as 'current,' where fatae—supernatural creatures—live and work alongside us, where magic, rather than fading in the modern world, thrives.

In 2011, after writing ten Cosa Nostradamus novels for Luna Books, and under contract for two more, my editor came to me and said "we think it's time to write something else. Not a Cosa novel."

I blinked, and thought about it, and decided that all right, I could do that. I had other story-ideas, after all, and ten books was a damn good run for a series, and...

And yet, the world of the Cosa Nostradamus refused to lay down and die, even as I was writing the new books for Luna. I'd promised to give Danny Hendrickson, my half-faun ex-cop PI his own adventures, after all, and Danny's not the kind of character you break a promise to.

(Seriously. He looks all boyish charm, but there's steel in his spine.)

But if my publisher thought there wasn't room for an eleventh novel...

Oh, screw it, I said. Brave new world! What New York thinks won't work is one thing, but what do you think?

I thought I wanted to write Danny's stories. And, I decided, if there was enough interest, I was damn well going to do so.

And so, I turned to Kickstarter and said "what do you think?" to potential backers.

They thought I should do it, too, raising enough money to write the two novellas you have in your hand, to pay for the editing and copyediting, the digital production and the cover design, and keep me (and the cats) fed long enough to get the stories written. And then people who'd missed the Kickstarter said "but wait! We want Danny stories, too!" And a small press said "we'd love to do the print edition, because we believe in the Cosa Nostradamus too!"

So with the blessing of my backers, I made the stories available to the public...

And that's why Sylvan Investigations exists: because—as PBS says—of readers like you. I hope you enjoyed it (and will come back for more!)

About the Author

Laura Anne Gilman is the author of the popular Cosa Nostradamus novels for Luna, and the Nebula award-nominated The *Vineart War* trilogy from Pocket, and a wide range of short fiction from many fine publishers.

In 2012 she dipped her pen into the mystery field as well, writing the *Gin & Tonic* series as L.A. Kornetsky.

Ms. Gilman is represented by Joe Monti at BGLA, and is a member of the writers' digital co-op Book View Café.

www.lauraannegilman.net

CPSIA information can be obtained at www.ICGtesting.com
Printed in the USA
BVOW04s0758120314

347414BV00001B/254/P